HER FOREVER MAN

HELLUVA ENGINEER, BOOK 3

SHIRLEY PENICK

HER FOREVER MAN

Photographer: Jean Woodfin

Cover Models: Tionna Petramalo and Robert Kelly

Contact me:

www.shirleypenick.com

www.facebook.com/ShirleyPenickAuthor

To sign up for Shirley's Monthly Newsletter, sign up on my website or send email to shirleypenick@outlook.com, subject newsletter.

CHAPTER 1

She was back! Lloyd Martin was surprised about how excited he was that Tracy Langley had returned to the ranch. He'd kept in touch with her over the four weeks, three days, and six hours she'd been gone, but seeing her again face to face was heaven. Pure heaven.

When she raced into his arms, he knew he was the luckiest man alive. He kissed her forehead and stepped back to give her the roses and candy he'd bought, since it *was* Valentine's Day.

She wore a heavy jacket and a cute snow hat, her long dark hair hanging down around her shoulders. Jeans and knee-high combat boots completed the outfit. Her nose ring today was a simple hoop and she only had two sets of earrings in, one hoops, that kind of matched the nose ring and a second set of studs. It was a very tame amount of jewelry for the woman who liked to flaunt fashion.

He wondered if it was in deference to her new job.

Her eyes still startled him, they were the lightest color of blue he'd ever seen, nearly clear. Even though he towered over her, he loved her hugs, it seemed like her curves exactly lined up to his body. A ridiculous thought, since she wasn't much more than five-foot and he'd passed six feet in high school.

He and Tracy weren't lovers, just really good friends, but he knew all women appreciated valentine-type gifts. He wouldn't be opposed to being more than friends, but she was too smart for the likes of him. Tracy was a grad student at one of the top engineering schools in the world, working on her PhD in Geology, and he'd just barely made it through high school.

They'd finally diagnosed his problem in his sophomore year, he had dyslexia. He knew how to manage it now, as an adult, but back then he'd just tried to hide the fact he couldn't read well, barely managing to get his diploma.

Tracy was way out of his league. But the two of them had become friends over the Christmas break when Tracy had come with a team of engineers to try to track the location of the gold mine that was causing contamination of the northern pasture of the Rockin' K ranch.

They'd found it too, and now she was back to work as an intern with the mine reclamation company that would be cleaning up the mine leavings. She was going to use the work for her PhD dissertation, then she'd be a full time Geological Engineer. He was so damn proud of her.

"Welcome back to the Rockin' K, Tracy. I missed your pretty face while you were gone. Here are some Valentine's Day gifts for my best girl."

She took his gifts and kissed his cheek, "I missed you too. I don't think I've ever gotten such nice V-day gifts, thanks, Lloyd."

"Let's grab your stuff and we can take it up to your room. You and Brenda will use the same rooms you had over Christmas."

"I brought a lot more stuff with me, since we'll be here full time for the semester. Brenda and I gave up our duplex, so other than what we put in storage, we brought it all, it will probably take a couple of trips to get it all inside."

She was babbling a bit, but he didn't mind. He liked the sound of her voice and she smelled so good. He'd be happy to spend the whole day toting and carrying for her, just to be near her.

He was thrilled at the idea of her being here for another four months or maybe even more, depending on how long the reclamation took. They wouldn't know that until the company engineers had a chance to fully assess the area. She would probably have to go back to school in the fall for her final year of graduate school, he didn't think internships lasted over one semester.

They grabbed everything they could carry and headed for the house. Tracy sighed. "It's great to be back. The air is so clear, the family is so nice, you're here, it's just perfect." She gave a little hop. "And I'll be getting paid. Not as much as I will later, when I have my diploma in my hand, but a whole lot more than I've ever made at any other job. I kind of feel like spinning and singing like Julie Andrews in the *Sound of Music*."

With a laugh he said, "After we get this first load in."

"I just can't quite believe it. I mean last semester I was struggling to pay the rent and now I have a job, a free place to stay with an incredible loving family. I'll be using my *paying* job as research for my thesis. It's the best feeling ever."

He grinned at her. "That's terrific. Congratulations on nailing it."

She shrugged. "I think it was more Steve and Patricia's doing than mine."

Lloyd knew Patricia was her school sponsor or mentor,

and Steve was Patricia's husband who had been a professional mine reclamation engineer for ten years before returning to his alma mater to teach, and marry Patricia. They had all come to the ranch over Christmas break to investigate the cause of contamination.

She continued speaking and he reigned in his thoughts to listen. "It could have also been Brenda's doing. They snapped her up the first day they were on campus for career day. I wasn't too far behind, but I still think one of them put a bug in their ear for me. I'm grateful for that."

"Well, whether they did or didn't mention you to them, I'm sure they wouldn't hire you, even as an intern, if you weren't the best candidate for the job. Then once you have those letters after your name, you'll be ready to take on the world."

She flashed him her killer smile, the one that made his heart stutter and warmth filled him.

It only took them three loads to bring in all her stuff and pile it in the middle of the bedroom floor. She was going to have a job to do to find a place for all of it. The Kiplings might have some storage she and Brenda could use if they needed it. Most of the boxes contained books and he assumed those were schoolbooks or reference manuals, although he knew she liked to read for pleasure, too.

TRACY COULDN'T BELIEVE HER BELONGINGS MADE SUCH A huge pile in her room. She didn't think she even owned so much. Being a foster kid most of her life didn't lend itself to a lot of possessions. But now that she was an adult, she'd been able to keep more things. Of course, half of that pile was books, but they were still hers.

She was thrilled to be back on the ranch and back with Lloyd. He and her roommate, Brenda, were the two people in her life who mattered the most. They were her only two real friends. The only two people who knew her completely and she felt safe with. She'd known Brenda for years now, they'd met and been roommates all through college. Brenda was a year ahead of her and would graduate in the spring. Tracy was not looking forward to being alone, but she was so happy for Brenda.

Lloyd on the other hand, she'd only known a handful of weeks, but they'd clicked from her very first day on the ranch. She was glad of that because Brenda had become enamored with Thomas and had been too busy with him to hang out with Tracy. Neither of them had ever really had an interest in boys prior, so she'd been surprised but not angry. They both wanted to get married someday, so it was probably coming to a time where they should start looking for that special guy, they were both hitting their thirties.

Tracy wondered if she could get Lloyd to help her unpack some of the boxes, or whether he had other ranch chores to do. She didn't want to give him up so soon after just getting here, and she would eat her cute snow hat if Brenda and Thomas weren't getting naked right about now. "Do you have time to give me a hand unpacking some of this?"

He looked at the pile and then back at her. "Sure, I can help. The boss cut us loose today to give you all a hand at settling in."

Not only was she happy to have his help, but she'd missed him the few weeks she'd been back at school. He was a good-looking man, tall, dark hair, blue eyes, and that was a nice plus, but his real value was how kind and understanding he was. He was peaceful to be around. "Awesome, if we could get the books organized that would cut the pile in half.

I'm so glad there are empty bookshelves. I'll be filling them and still have some overflow."

Lloyd's smile was crooked. "I don't doubt that for a minute. We might be able to confiscate another bookshelf or two from the other empty bedrooms."

"Do you think so? Won't they be missed?"

"The rooms sit empty nearly one-hundred percent of the time. If we took the shelves from Adam or Beau's room, we should be fine. We can ask of course, but I can't imagine anyone would care, Beau and Adam both have their own homes only a few yards away."

She'd seen the other houses and yes, they were close, but further than a few yards. Still if no one was using the rooms or bookshelves, maybe... She looked at the shelves and decided if they were going to bring another one in it would be best to do before they started filling the one already in the room.

"All right, if you don't think they would mind."

"We'll just grab what we need and then discuss it later."

Tracy felt like a thief as they looked in both the empty rooms. But she didn't hesitate to help Lloyd carry the two bookshelves, from what had been Beau's room, into her own.

When they got the shelves arranged along one wall, Lloyd stood back and then looked at the boxes of books. "Those might hold them all, but I'm not going to bet on it."

"We'll just have to make them fit."

Lloyd grinned. "Let's get after it then."

He did all the unboxing and heavy lifting, while she arranged the books the way she wanted them. Each box was a new adventure, as she worked to fit them on the shelves in an order that made sense and would be the easiest for her home-work or research.

Some of the boxes had been in storage, since their duplex

had been on the small side, and she and Brenda had had a lot of duplicates. But they'd decided that it would be better not to leave them in storage on the other side of the continental divide, so they'd packed them into the car. They'd left furniture and kitchen appliances in storage, knowing they didn't need those while they were on the ranch and living in the family home.

"I think this is the last book box, the rest look like clothes and shoes and stuff," Lloyd said.

"That's good because I'm running out of shelf space."

He opened the box. "Oh, it's novels, not textbooks."

Her smile lit up the room and she rushed to him. "Good, I was hoping that box hadn't gotten lost. It's all the books I collected before going to college." She started to look through the books and suddenly there were tears clogging her throat and burning her eyes. It was the box of her most prized possessions. The one and only box she ever took with her from foster home to foster home, or girl's home.

She took the box from his hands and went back to the bookshelf before she started crying. She cleared her throat and said, "Maybe you should go ask about us confiscating the shelves."

He ran one hand down her hair, probably reading right through her. "I'll do that, might need to check in with the boss too, just to make sure. I'll be back in a bit to see if you need more help."

She didn't answer, just nodded, and heard the door softly click as he left her alone to get herself together.

CHAPTER 2

*L*loyd leaned back against Tracy's door for a moment, she'd looked so beautiful when her eyes had filled. Beautiful and shattered at the same time. His heart had broken for the little girl she'd been. She'd told him about her former life, when she'd been at the ranch during the Christmas holiday. She'd been so overwhelmed by the generosity of the Kipling family, she'd broken down a couple of times, and he'd held her while she cried.

When she hadn't turned toward him this time, he realized she wanted to be alone, to compose herself. It disappointed him. He was very willing to offer her comfort, but some things were too deep and painful to share.

He took the stairs down to see if he could find someone to ask about the bookshelves. He already knew what they would say, but Tracy would feel more secure once he had the confirmation.

He couldn't imagine what she'd gone through as a child, his dad and grandpa had always been there for him. He didn't remember his mom much; she'd died when he was only four. But he'd always had his father. His dad might have done some kind of odd things, like going off to try for fame and fortune by gold mining, but he'd always had Lloyd's back even with his learning disability.

His dad hadn't been much of a reader, or his grandpa, once Lloyd was diagnosed, they'd realized they all had the same disability. It hadn't helped him read any better, but it had given him back some self-esteem.

Lloyd found Grandpa K in the living room, sitting by the fire with a ranching magazine in his hand. The man looked up and Lloyd could see the devilment in the old man's eyes. "Have you been helping those pretty girls get settled?"

"Yes, sir. Tracy anyway, Thomas was helping Brenda."

Grandpa K nodded, but Lloyd could practically see the man's thoughts. "I'm sure he's doing a fine job getting Brenda settled."

Brenda and Thomas had gotten a lot cozier during their time together over the break, than he and Tracy. It had been Brenda's doing for the most part, Lloyd thought. He let a tiny smirk flit over his lips before he pulled his wayward thoughts back. "Tracy brought a lot more things with her this time. A whole ton of books."

"Makes sense. I heard they would both be taking some online classes while working at the mine."

"Yeah, they're going to be busy. Anyway, we got a couple of bookshelves out of Beau's room to help store all of her books. Do you think that's going to be a problem?"

"Not at all. In fact, I heard Meg mention she'd like to spruce up both rooms, so having less bookshelves in the way would make that easier. My daughter-in-law will probably thank you for paving the way, or maybe my son. Travis is not a fan of moving furniture around. Not that he'd have any choice in the matter, gotta keep the misses happy," he chuckled.

Lloyd thought back to the rooms, and while he thought they looked fine, he could see her maybe wanting to de-male the rooms. Having five boys in the house didn't let her decorate much, but now that they were all married and had built homes of their own, she was free to do as she liked.

"Glad we could be of service. I'll have Tracy let Brenda know she can confiscate the one in Adam's room. Thanks, Grandpa K. I'll go put Tracy's mind at ease."

He knocked on the door and when she opened it with a smile, he knew she'd pulled herself together. "Grandpa K says Meg is wanting to redecorate and will be glad to hear the bookshelves are no longer in the way. You might tell Brenda she can have the other one."

He looked at the bookshelves and saw she'd put away the last box. The compass Grandpa K had given her, and the picture of Tony were both in places of honor. It choked him up a bit to see those items she'd saved from her time here on the ranch, displaying them proudly. He cleared his throat. "Looks like you won't need it."

"Everything fits perfectly, she can have the last one."

There was music playing, not loudly but not as quiet as he would have thought. It made him curious.

TRACY WAS GLAD LLOYD HAD GIVEN HER A FEW MINUTES alone, although taking his comfort had been her first response, but she'd pulled that back. She needed to stand on her own two feet. There wasn't going to be a man around every time she felt sad, nostalgic, or overwhelmed, best to get used to that now.

Except for the fact that Lloyd leaving had left a silence that allowed her to hear Brenda and Thomas, together in

Brenda's room. Tracy wasn't a prude, but she didn't necessarily want to listen to what she was pretty sure she was hearing. So, she'd shut the door to the connecting bathroom and had turned on music.

She breathed a sigh of relief when Lloyd came back to distract her from her roommate's enthusiastic return to the Rockin' K ranch, and Thomas.

They set up her study area next, computer, printer, notebooks, and other study paraphernalia. They got her hooked up to the house internet and she was ready to go. About the only thing left was clothes and personal stuff, so Lloyd left her to that, and went to see if he was needed elsewhere.

As he was leaving, she gave him a huge hug. "Thanks for all your help, it would have taken me a couple of days to get that all done by myself."

He shrugged in his self-deprecating way. "I'm always happy to help a pretty woman who needs a strong back. I'll see you at supper. I think the rest of your crew will be there."

Was she just any pretty woman? She kind of hoped she was at least a little special to him. But maybe her foolish heart was running away with her, she needed to rein it in. "Yes, they will. And thanks for the flowers and candy, too. What a great Valentine's Day it's been."

Lloyd just grinned at her and then shut her door. Tracy knew she had a sappy smile on her face, but she was all alone, so didn't care one bit. He was so much more than a strong back. He was a hard worker and was respected by his peers, and the owners of the ranch. He was also kind and gentle with her when she needed kindness, but didn't coddle her the rest of the time.

She'd heard enough to know he had a reading disability, but he was far from ignorant, he'd followed along with their conversations about the mine and contamination. He'd even seemed to understand the geology behind how they were tracking the gold vein. She'd wondered about that, until Christmas Eve, and then even through her own trauma about those gifts, she'd noticed that his book gift was an audio book.

Tracy had asked him how many audio books he owned.

"Oh, not that many, they are pretty expensive. I can get them online through the library system. There are enough fiction books in audio to last two or three lifetimes. If I find something that's not converted to audio, I can use the e-book for it with a read along device. The voice is boring and pretty monotone, but if I want to learn something, I can."

She'd thought about that and wondered if some of her textbooks, that were the most necessary, were in e-book form, she didn't need audio, but having some of her prized reference books on her phone would be amazing. She'd looked them up and sure enough a couple of them were. At Christmas she hadn't been able to afford them, but she planned to buy some, now that she would have an income.

The idea of having an income while still in school made her want to do the happy dance. She'd gotten so tired of always being a financial drain on Brenda. Not that Brenda felt that way, the woman had a trust fund that wouldn't quit, and completely absent parents. Tracy had met them once, individually, since they had divorced and were enjoying other people. Tracy had felt more affection in the foster homes she'd been in than with either of Brenda's parents.

Money obviously didn't buy love, that was certain.

She was finished putting away the last box. She broke them down with her field knife and stacked them, before she shoved them under the bed. Her room looked terrific, she was organized and ready for her first day on the job, tomorrow. And she was organized for her online classes as well.

It was still a while until dinner, so after flopping on her bed and admiring her room, she decided maybe she could be useful to this family who had been so kind to her. After a shower and clothes change, she went down into the kitchen to see if she could be of use. That would also leave the bathroom open for Brenda.

Tracy hoped Lloyd would be waiting for her, but he did have other jobs on the ranch besides working with the engineers, so she kept her expectations low. She always tried to keep her expectations low, so she didn't end up being disappointed. It wasn't a very positive way to live, but it wasn't as hurtful either. She'd tried to be positive, but it just never worked for her. So, she'd given up a long time ago and gone into protective mode.

CHAPTER 3

*M*eg, the matriarch of the large family, grinned when Tracy walked into the kitchen. "Well now look at this, I have two helpers tonight." Meg was a pretty woman in her early fifties, who made everyone feel at home in her house. Tracy hoped she could grow up to be just like her.

Lloyd was chopping cucumbers, tomatoes, and other vegetables to spruce up the bag of salad. He gave Tracy a quick wink and went back to chopping.

"Lloyd and I were so efficient getting all my belongings put away that I'm done putting my room to rights. Did Lloyd tell you about relocating the shelves out of Beau's room?"

"He did indeed, and I am pleased as punch, both because you can put them to good use and because it opens up the room so I can redecorate."

"Goody, so now I'm at your service, what do you have for me to help with?"

Meg, who was manning the stove in an apron that had seen a lot of meals cooked, said, "I'd let you mash the potatoes."

Tracy laughed thinking of Meg's young grandson. "Hopefully I can do as good of a job as Tony. I kind of miss him."

Meg pushed the strand of dark brown hair out of her face. "I more than kind of miss him, it's like all the energy has left the house with that boy. But I got to have him for five years, and now it's Zach's turn."

Tracy had heard the story of how it had come to be that Zach hadn't known Emma's son was his own. It was a crazy set of coincidences that no one could have imagined, let alone engineered. "Yeah, but this house seems so empty. It's made for lots of people like we had at Christmas."

Meg smiled as her eyes shimmered. "Believe me, I get it. It's hard having this big house with all the kids gone. I like having you and Brenda around to help fill up the rooms."

Tracy didn't want to get both her and Meg bawling so she changed the subject. "Didn't your kids help a lot with the cooking?"

"Yes, I insisted each of them cook a meal one day a week, so they all learned how to cook. I did want them to learn, but it also gave me a break," Meg said with a laugh. "With just the three of us in the house these days the cooking falls on me, but it's not very extensive. Three servings is really no big deal and we're pretty easy to please. But it's fun when there are more people about."

Tracy said, "Brenda and I could help with some of the cooking on the days we aren't out in the field. We aren't the best cooks, since neither of us learned how when we were younger. Not until we got our own apartment off campus, then we had to learn the hard way. But we finally managed to learn enough not to have to order pizza every day."

Meg said, "And it also makes it hard to learn when you've got no one to show you."

"Yeah, we watched a lot of online videos and cooking

shows. I envy your kids having you train them. Even Tony knows how to mash potatoes, mostly." Tracy remembered the mashed potatoes Tony had made over Christmas, they'd been edible, but just barely.

"He's gotten so much better, the first time when he was only five, was a disaster. But not one person said so. It was amusing to watch. I think they were all thinking back to their own first attempts at cooking and what semi-disasters those had been."

Tracy and Lloyd exchanged glances and grinned. Tracy knew that everyone had been kind to Tony because they loved the boy, and no one would want to hurt his feelings. He was adorable and was currently off with his mom and dad on the rodeo circuit.

He'd probably be back from time to time when they weren't competing. Tracy hoped she'd see him, she didn't know much about the rodeo circuit or when they had time off, except over Christmas.

As Tracy mashed the potatoes, she noticed Meg keeping an eye on her. When it was time to add the milk, Meg suggested using cream instead. When she was nearly done and the potatoes were creamy, Meg had her put nearly a half-pound of butter in them and stir that in good.

Meg gave her a tasting spoon and Tracy had to admit they were the best potatoes she'd ever had, except she thought they could use a pinch of salt. Tracy looked up to see Meg handing her a salt mill. With a grin she added the sea salt and mixed it all up one more time, then dumped it into a serving bowl

Lloyd and Tracy carried out their offerings, while Travis, Meg's husband, came in to carry out the meat. Brenda and Thomas breezed in looking freshly scrubbed and thoroughly relaxed, they carried in the gravy and fruit bowl, leaving Meg with the vegetables and rolls.

Thomas said, "Brenda and I will take cleanup, since we didn't make it down to lend a hand earlier."

Meg patted him on the shoulder with a knowing smile on her face. "That would be nice."

When they were all seated around the table, Travis introduced the rest of the engineering team to the others that hadn't met them yet. Then he led the group in a short blessing for the food and the serving bowls started passing.

LLOYD FOUND DINNER TO BE A LITTLE DISCONCERTING. IT seemed that no one really knew each other. Tracy and Brenda obviously knew the Kipling family and him and Thomas. But they didn't know the engineers at all. The engineers didn't know them either. There were four men. Two of them had brought wives, one, Connor, had brought some older kids, probably ten and twelve.

The kids seemed unfazed by being at a table with a bunch of strangers, which he felt was unusual. Then again, if the engineers went around to all kinds of locations and took their children with them, it wouldn't be a big surprise that the kids were adaptable.

Travis said, "We'll have another dinner in a couple of days where we'll bring the rest of the family that live and work on the land. We didn't want to force a group dinner on Valentine's Day. Our sons haven't been married very long and need to continue to show their wives their appreciation. So, we decided that we'd let them woo their wives for Valentine's Day."

Connor, the older man with the children laughed. "Yeah, the first few years you got to keep your eye on that."

His wife, Marci, looked at him with a raised eyebrow. "Just the first few years?"

The man made a harumphing sound and then started back pedaling. "No, not at all, honey. Gotta keep doing it. But we had our Valentine's Day earlier today, didn't we?"

She said, "I suppose."

Cyrus, a young boy who looked to be about twelve, swallowed and pointed with his fork. "Hey, you had breakfast in bed while Sissy and I had cold cereal."

Marci smiled and cut a piece of meat. "That we did, and it was very pleasant. I can't complain. Plus, you had the trailer all ready for us to go, honey. Even stocked with food so I'm quite happy with my valentine."

Travis winked at Meg and put a large fork of potatoes in his mouth. Lloyd took that to mean that maybe Meg and Travis had had breakfast in bed as well. Before the crowds arrived.

Grandpa K asked, "So what's the plan, now that you're all here?"

Connor, who was clearly the lead for the team, tapped his fork on his plate. "We'll start with measurements, both the size of the containment field and the amount of cyanide and other contaminants found in it. Mercury was used back in the day, so we'll be checking for that as well. And anything that can be harvested with contemporary methods, we know a lot more than they did back then."

He took another bite of potatoes while that sunk in around the table. "We'll also want to check the land straight downhill from the mine to make sure there isn't another area below it with contamination. It might be that there is more than one area that needs cleaning up. Especially if it's as old of a mine as you think it might be. We might be able to do some testing along those lines, to pinpoint the age of the original mine and also when the recent activity that gave you the trouble, took place."

Grandpa K nodded. "That would be helpful. Pinpointing the most recent trouble would give us some good data. The date of the original mine would be interesting, but I don't see how it would matter now."

Lloyd set down his fork. "Unless we can determine who mined it originally. Then look at the family tree to see who might be looking at it now."

Grandpa K rubbed his chin in consideration. "Good point Lloyd, as far as we know, the mine never had a claim put in on it. But more information is certainly better than less."

Connor continued, "Once we determine the concentration of the cyanide and anything else we find, and determine what microbes are already at work, we'll know more how to treat it. Regardless of what we find, I can't see this taking any less than six months to clean up. Unfortunately, we have to be careful not to cause more problems with a too aggressive approach."

Meg smiled, "Working with Mother Nature is a delicate balance." She lifted the meat platter. "Would anyone like seconds?"

A few of them did take more food and after everyone was served, Travis said, "I've assigned you Thomas and Lloyd to help out with anything you need. They've both lived and worked on the ranch for years, so if you have any questions, they should know the answers. Will you need any other help?"

"Not at first, we'll do what needs to be done and bring in any expertise needed. Once the initial assessment is done and the scientific work is complete, we could use some help with the physical labor part of the operation. We'll cover the land with a deep layer of soil, and plant trees, shrubs, and grasses over it. At that stage we can either hire out the work or use your staff. But that's a few months out at this point, so just something to keep in mind for later. It'll need to be after the last hard frost, a good time for planting."

Travis nodded, "Good to know, when we get closer to a date we'll decide. In the meantime, Thomas and Lloyd are at your command. And as I mentioned when we took the trailers out by cabin two, you can hook up to the water and electricity out there. Anything else you need, just give a holler."

Lloyd worked not to smile as he thought back to when Travis had first assigned him to work with the engineers. He'd been totally irritated. Yes, he'd been on gold mining sites in the past and yes, he had some idea of what went on. He hadn't been an adult back then, however, he'd still been a kid. And he figured what he did learn had probably changed in the years since he'd been on a mining site.

When Travis had told them the engineers were coming for Christmas, he'd listened to a lot of podcasts, had gotten some books from the library. He'd picked up some information and he figured he knew a few things, but nothing like the engineers would know. He'd feel stupid and he hated that. So, he'd had an attitude about being assigned to the stupid gold mine project here at the ranch. He was an adult, so he hadn't let it show, but he'd felt it. Right up until the engineers from the front range had arrived a week before Christmas.

The two cars had driven into the parking area. And he'd walked up next to Thomas who was running the show with the engineers. He didn't think Thomas knew Lloyd was supposed to be helping, but that was okay, he wasn't in any hurry to admit that. But he figured he'd better help with the luggage at the very least.

The older engineer pointed toward the Land Rover and said that the luggage was inside. Just about that time, the two girls exited the front of the car. There was a blonde and a brunette. And they both stretched after the long car ride. The brunette caught his eye. She was so pretty.

And when she stretched and her shirt pulled up, he saw just a sliver of skin. He knew he was done for. That sliver of skin did something to his brain. Practically shut it down. He wasn't the brightest crayon in the box to begin with, so having all his blood rush from his head to his nether regions did not help in any way.

He'd just stood there looking at the beautiful dark-haired girl. Tracy and he had become fast friends and he'd learned to stifle the lust. But every once in a while, it tried to resurface.

Meg brought him out of his memories when she asked if anyone was ready for dessert. Lloyd never passed on dessert; he had a powerful sweet tooth.

CHAPTER 4

Tracy dressed for the Colorado high country weather. It might look sunny and warm out her bedroom window, but it was February, in the mountains, where the plains started at a mile high, and the ranch elevation was close to nine-thousand feet. They could get three feet of snow, or not one flake, it could be below zero out or a balmy fifty degrees, the most likely temperature would be around freezing. Sunshine did not equal warm, in fact, some of the coldest days were bright and clear.

So, she pulled on the clothes she and Brenda had purchased from the sporting goods store, before they'd come up here at Christmas break. In truth Brenda had bought everything, which still felt weird to Tracy. She'd drug her feet on Brenda buying so much stuff. Their list was not a short one. Brenda was a Silver Spoon baby, so she always had the nicest equipment, her parents didn't give a fuck about her, but she had a good car, and plenty of money.

Brenda had happily dragged her through the sporting goods store piling two shopping carts full of clothes and equipment. Hiking boots, snow boots, long thermal underwear, down jackets, snow pants, and vests, hats and gloves, and even face masks, the kind that she'd only seen on people robbing a store. On top of that, Brenda also got all the things they would need in case any weather dumped on them and they were stranded in snow. Brenda had nearly needed to use those things their second day on the ranch, when an unpredicted snowstorm had come through the area. Fortunately, Thomas had found her, and they'd stayed the night in cabin two.

Tracy had to admit she was glad to have every single item Brenda had forced on her. Before they'd come here this time, they'd gone back to the sporting goods store and loaded up on more winter clothes. They were going to be spending months here, not three weeks like before.

Brenda came into her room through the joint bathroom, apparently Thomas had gone on before. "You ready?"

"Yep, I feel a little like a stuffed animal, but better that, than cold."

"Totally agree with you on that one. Having to pee is going to take a week, if I wasn't dead set on coffee, I wouldn't bother with liquids at all," Brenda said shuffling toward the door.

"I hear you, but I hope we have a thermos full to take with us."

"Agreed."

Not wanting to stay in the house in all their winter clothing, the girls grabbed some coffee in to-go cups, and breakfast burritos. Whoever had decided to add tortillas to the breakfast spread was a genius. They walked out munching on their foil wrapped burritos to find the extended cab truck with two large snowmobiles attached to a trailer.

The bed of the truck held snowshoes, a large thermos of coffee, and a bunch of other stuff. Tracy had no idea what they would need all of that stuff for, but she trusted Lloyd and Thomas to know more about it than she did.

Thomas and Brenda took the front seat and Tracy and Lloyd the back.

Brenda asked, "What's with all the equipment?"

Thomas shrugged. "A lot of it we'll store in the mine cave or the barn at cabin two, the snowmobiles we'll use as transportation up and down the mountain. Since we know where we're going it will be easier than using the horses or hiking. The snowshoes we'll also keep with us."

"Why the snowshoes?" Tracy asked.

"Connor said last night he wanted to check downhill. If the snow is still fresh and powdery, they will help keep us on top of the snow. We got several feet of it after the new year."

Tracy couldn't figure out how they were going to find any additional areas if everything was under two feet of snow, but that's why she was the student. She would no doubt find out soon.

When they got to cabin two, they unloaded the truck, Tracy and Brenda putting things where they were instructed. As they worked, the jumble of equipment started to make sense. Lanterns, mostly battery powered, but two that used propane, would be handy on gloomy days or in the mine's cave. A couple of Coleman stoves, cooking equipment, including a cast iron coffee pot, and food to cook on them, which they planned to take to the cave to use as emergency rations if snow moved in and cut them off.

Sleeping bags and thermal gear would also be left in the cave, along with some portable heaters. It seemed like they were planning to get snowed in. Tracy wasn't a fan of that idea. "Do you really think we're going to get snowed in up there?"

Lloyd shook his head. "No, but better safe than sorry.

Plan for disaster and hope you can haul it all back down unused."

Tracy smiled at him. "Got it, and I hope we do haul it all down unused."

"You and me both."

LLOYD HOPED HE'D ALLEVIATED TRACY'S FEARS, BUT HE knew it was entirely possible they could get stranded on the mountain. February through April were the most dangerous months, where they could be dumped on with very little warning.

He and Thomas had planned it out last night with Travis, after the engineers had left. Cabin two and their trailers would be good and safe if they got down the mountain. If not, they could hunker down in the cave for up to a week or even two, if necessary.

Fortunately, the reclamation company employees and seasoned engineers had brought similar equipment. They also had two snowmobiles. That made four total, and each would hold two people, so those would work to get the eight of them up and down the mountain, leaving the ranch's other snow-mobiles for tending the cattle.

After everything was unloaded and stored in the mine, they split up into two teams, each with a seasoned engineer at the head. Connor's team walked the perimeter of the mine tailings that Patricia and Brenda had mapped out. He took the other junior engineer, Frank, Brenda, and Thomas with him to start gathering more samples from the area.

Matt, the other senior engineer, took his team into the cave. They explored the formation of quartz that encased the vein of gold. Tracy and Lloyd were in that group, and he soon discovered that a lot of the focus was on teaching the younger engineers how to examine the rock and explaining exactly what they were looking for. Which was a lot more complicated than what Lloyd had imagined.

They looked at the rocks to try to determine how they had been mined. What kind of instruments had been used. Modern day equipment left a slightly different pattern. It was fascinating. Apparently, Matt was charged with dating the mine and finding where the modern work had started. Lloyd wondered if Matt was a Geologist, like Tracy would be, rather than a reclamation engineer, like Brenda. Lloyd found the information fascinating and since he had two good eyes, he was allowed to join the examination.

He found something that didn't quite look right, so he called Tracy over. She agreed with him and went to get Matt.

Matt had gathered the other engineer to come look also. "What did you find Lloyd?"

He wasn't thrilled about the whole team descending, but sucked in a breath. "This looks odd to me. I don't know what it means, but it's different."

Matt leaned in and looked at the spot for several minutes before pulling out the mini-magnifier, Lloyd knew they called a hand lens. Without saying a word, he handed the hand lens to the younger engineer Julian. "What do you make of that Julian?"

"Um, well it looks like Kalgoorlie."

"Very good, and why would we care about that particular mineral?"

"It's often host to gold, especially in the Cripple Creek area and Boulder County."

"Exactly, and we are not too far removed from both of those locales. It's possible the previous miners had no idea what it was, it might have been wiser to follow that rather than the skinny vein of gold in the quartz."

He slapped Lloyd on the back. "Good work."

Tracy beamed at him; Lloyd felt his cheeks heat.

Matt asked Tracy, "Did you know what it was?"

"I suspected, which is why I came to find you."

"You two make a good team. Let's flag that and keep moving, still a lot of cave to examine. Keep your eyes open for other tellurides associated with gold, and silver is also a good possibility."

They continued searching. Another discovery of silver was found, but it looked small. Someone had followed it for a short while, making a cavity in the walls, but then turned back. Gold had been more lucrative than silver even then. They flagged that location, too.

At one point toward the back of the cave Matt had called them to join him. "What do you see here?"

Lloyd probably was supposed to stay silent, but he simply couldn't. "The scrapings look brighter, fresher, and have the more modern tool patterns."

"Excellent Lloyd, you would make a fine engineer. You're very observant."

He muttered, "Thanks," and hoped the guy would move on.

But Matt proved to be tenacious. "Our company would sponsor you to get your degree, but then you would have to come work for us for the rest of your natural life." He laughed at his own joke.

Lloyd didn't want to admit he couldn't read in front of an audience, so was breathless with thankfulness when Conner showed up at the mouth of the cave. "Hey, you guys, it's lunch time, come on out in the sunshine, soak up some vitamin D."

Lloyd and Matt hung back while the other two made a beeline for the cave mouth. Lloyd said, "I appreciate your enthusiasm, but I can't read. I have dyslexia."

"But you've been right up to date on all the methods."

"I get audio books and have an audio reader on my phone and laptop, so when I want to know something, I study up that way. I've been learning about mine reclamation since Christmas, so I could follow along with the conversations."

"Well, you may not be able to read, but you've got a fine mind in there. The college might have a program you would fit into."

Lloyd didn't want Matt to stir up trouble. "Naw, I'm just a cowboy."

"If you say so," Matt said, but Lloyd wasn't sure the subject was closed.

CHAPTER 5

*T*racy noticed Lloyd was quieter than normal the rest of the day, and blamed Matt on his insistence that Lloyd go to college. She didn't know if Lloyd had told Matt about his learning disability or not. She didn't like seeing Lloyd withdraw and hoped he wasn't embarrassed. He'd done a damn fine job of educating himself and didn't need some guy forcing his views on him. And she didn't give a damn if the guy was one of her bosses, she might just give him a piece of her mind.

She wanted to talk to Lloyd about it and see how he felt, but when they returned to the house, he made excuses and hurried off toward the bunk house. They weren't having any kind of special meal together so she wouldn't see him again until morning. She thought about a text but that didn't allow her to see his face.

In the kitchen there was food on the stove with a sign that read 'Help Yourself', it smelled delicious, but she just couldn't deal with food right now her stomach was in knots. She just kept walking and trudged up the stairs to her room with Brenda right behind her.

Brenda asked, "Hey what's going on, did you and Lloyd have a fight or something? You both seemed out of sorts at lunch and then again tonight."

Tracy didn't know if she should discuss this whole thing with Brenda, but she knew she wouldn't settle until she did, so she dragged her friend into the room and locked the door. "No, Lloyd and I are fine. It was Matt that caused the problem."

"How so?" Brenda asked as she stripped out of most of her clothes, until she was down to the thermal underwear, then she flopped onto Tracy's bed.

Tracy finished pulling off her outerwear too, but was too keyed up to sit, so she paced while she told Brenda about their morning. How Lloyd had found several important discoveries in the mine walls and how impressed Matt had been by him finding them.

"But all that sounds wonderful, why aren't you both excited?"

"Because after those discoveries Matt started telling Lloyd he should go on to school and get either a degree or certification and join the company."

"Oh no! What happened then?"

"You called us out for lunch. Lloyd waited with Matt, and I assume they talked about Lloyd's reading disability. I don't know for sure because Lloyd pretty much closed down after that."

"Oh man. That sucks! Here Lloyd is doing a good job helping and Matt has to butt his nose in."

Tracy sat on her bed next to her friend and leaned in for a one-armed hug. "Now I don't know if I should say something to Matt. I want to give him a piece of my mind, but he really was trying to be helpful."

"Yeah, plus the whole boss thing."

"Exactly. I also don't know if I should try to talk to Lloyd, he clearly shut me out this afternoon. Maybe he was embarrassed, but I know all about his dyslexia and how he works around it, so he shouldn't be ashamed around me."

"Maybe he's just thinking it through. Sometimes we all need thinking time."

Tracy hoped that was the case and he'd be fine tomorrow. "That would be good. He knows he can call me if he wants to talk about it."

"I'm sure he will. Now let's put on some real clothes and go get some of that dinner Meg left us. I'm starving."

Tracy smiled. "It did smell delicious. You're a good friend, Brenda."

"I know. I passed by food to talk. But now I'm getting dressed."

Tracy hugged herself as her friend gathered up all the work clothes and scurried to her room. She did have a wonderful friend in Brenda. She thought of Lloyd and wished she knew the right thing to do there.

Dinner ended up being her, Brenda, and Grandpa K. Grandpa K asked them about the day's activities. Tracy told him about Lloyd finding some interesting things in the mine that had not been discovered previously.

Grandpa K rubbed his chin. "I always knew that boy had smarts. His observation skills have always been keen. He's also learned to overcome his learning challenges. I think Matt has a good idea, suggesting he could do more. If Matt pushes though, Lloyd will shut down."

Tracy agreed with that.

He chuckled. "Us ranchers are a stubborn bunch. Just give Lloyd some room on it and let him ponder it a bit. I'll put a bug in Matt's ear to just let the idea simmer. Might let Travis in on the idea."

"Thanks Grandpa K. I'll leave it in your hands. And now I have some homework to attend to." Tracy felt so much better, she'd been a little surprised that Grandpa K had agreed with Matt. If Lloyd did decide to pursue it, they would lose a good ranch hand. Then again, the Kipling family wasn't the type to hold anyone back, that was in evidence with Drew being a sheriff in Wyoming, and Emma being on the rodeo circuit with her husband.

Letting it all go, she opened her laptop and got to work, but the idea niggled that if Lloyd did pursue it and went to work for the same company she did, maybe she and Lloyd could have a different future from the one she'd imagined. Maybe they could be more than friends. Not a good reason for him to make the change, maybe, but an intriguing thought just the same.

LLOYD WENT INTO HIS ROOM AND REALIZED HE DIDN'T really need to change out of his work clothes, other than to remove the extra layers, he didn't get as dirty working with the engineers as he did as a ranch hand. That saved on laundry, he'd noticed that when they'd been here over Christmas. He would still help with the evening chores, if needed, but that was usually light work.

He stripped out of his long-johns as he contemplated his ideas for the evening. He was definitely going to look up the rocks he'd discovered today, the Kalgoorlie and tellurides and other information he could find on other gold mines found in Colorado.

He'd also decided to look up mine reclamation certification, he didn't want a four-year degree but if there was a few months program, he might be able to handle a few classes. He didn't want anyone to know about that idea, though, not even Thomas.

Lloyd looked up what could be found near gold deposits, especially in Colorado. He found a book in the library system that focused on gold and silver finds in the area and checked out the e-book version of it. He wondered if the engineers would let him take a small sample to examine, he'd ordered a hand lens that would arrive in a few days.

He did one quick search on mine reclamation certification. There were some programs, but then he'd have to leave the ranch and he didn't think he wanted to do that. He shut that browser window down with a firm decision not to pursue it.

Before he'd closed the window, he'd noticed one program that offered certification that was in the town where Tracy's school was. She'd be going back next year and had mentioned she wasn't excited about being alone, since Brenda was graduating. Before he could stop himself, he imagined Tracy and himself in a little house together. It was an appealing vision, but also ridiculous, so he shut his mind down the same way as he had the browser window.

But damn, the idea felt so right.

CHAPTER 6

*T*racy and Lloyd were the last two at the mine. Tracy was working on a project and wanted to finish it before they went down. It was the weekend. They weren't planning to work on Saturday or Sunday. So, she just wanted to finish up gathering the samples so she could play with them over the weekend, she had a geology degree but was enjoying the reclamation side, looking at the microbes and how they were affecting the contamination.

She slipped her last sample vial into the carrying case she and Brenda had found at the outfitter's store. There had been a sign for some weird sport they'd never heard of, and they'd been curious, so they'd gone over to see the stuff used for that. One of the things they'd found was what they were using as a sample case. It was the perfect design for holding test tubes for specimens. It was a metal case lined with foam and held twelve test tubes, all safely nestled to keep them safe from damage.

They'd shown it to their mentors who had quickly gone and bought themselves one. Even on this assignment when they'd pulled them out to use them Connor had immediately noticed and examined Brenda's before getting on his phone and having their office manager order one for everyone in the field. She and Brenda had scored major brownie points for innovation.

She was glad she'd finished collecting all the samples, as it was getting toward dusk. Dark fell quickly in the mountains, and they didn't like coming down without the light. There was a headlamp on the snowmobile, and they had a decent track to follow, but it was still smarter to get down before the sun was down.

As she knelt and gathered up her rock hammer and sample case there was a strange rumble above her. She stood to see if she could get a look at what it was. A wall of snow hit her knees and knocked her feet out from under her. Shit was this an avalanche? Her mind raced, she didn't want to get swept downhill, maybe if she grabbed that tree and hung on, she wouldn't be. She crawled on her belly up to it, one of her legs was giving out, she used her rock hammer to give her leverage, using the point to dig in.

She managed to get one arm around the tree and then a second as the snow tore at her, trying to drag her down the hill. She dropped her sample case and clung as the white stuff covered her. She'd read something about an avalanche and the main reason people died in them was suffocation, she tried to make a cocoon between her and the tree, where there was air instead of snow.

Praying Lloyd would find her she lay flat on her stomach as the ice and snow covered her. She wanted to sob but stopped herself, she had to listen for Lloyd. She breathed as shallowly as she could, nearly holding her breath, she had to listen. What seemed like hours, but had probably only been a few minutes, she heard him call out to her.

He was coming to save her, she pulled in enough breath to

answer him, hoping it wouldn't be her last. "Lloyd, I'm here, by the tree."

He sounded so far away and muffled but she understood him. He needed her to make noise, but not use up her oxygen. Her rock hammer, but what could she hit it on to make noise? She felt around, no rocks, just snow and the tree. She wanted to cry, but then her hand grazed her sample case. With profound relief she knew that would work.

Getting the two of them together when she could hardly move took her a minute, but then the sound of freedom started ringing in her ears. It was loud in her prison of snow, but she was sure Lloyd would be able to hear it.

Continuing to breathe in shallow pants she beat on her sample case with the flat side of her rock hammer. Over and over until she felt Lloyd touch her back. Relief flooded her. Her head was still covered, so she wasn't out of the woods yet, but it wouldn't be long now, Lloyd wouldn't let her die in this snowy world.

He was her hero and she wondered why she'd never made love to him. She could have died never knowing. She'd seen lust flair in his eyes, and she'd felt it too, so why...

"Are you all right? Are you hurt?"

She took in a huge breath and turned her head enough to see the man that had saved her. After a short conversation he got busy. He still had to uncover her legs so as he did that, she thought about how to seduce him. She'd been spared and she was going to grab that man with both hands. They might not have forever together, but they had the next few months, she was by God, not going to waste them.

LLOYD WAS INSIDE THE MINE WHEN THE RUMBLE STARTED. He'd finally gotten up the courage and asked if he could have a small sample of the silver and the tellurides. They'd been perfectly fine with that idea, so he was getting that sample out of the rock. He'd finally gotten the second piece when he heard a strange, rumbling sound. It almost sounded like a strong wind, or a minor rockslide. But it had been a windless day, and everything was covered in snow. There were no clouds.

He rushed to the front of the cave and saw snow. Lots of snow. It was an avalanche. And Tracy was out in it.

He called out, "Tracy, Tracy!"

But he was certain she wouldn't be able to hear him over the rumble of the snow. He forced himself to stay in the cave, rather than rushing out. He wouldn't be able to help her if he was swept down the mountain. He hoped she hadn't been carried away. He prayed she was close. It didn't take long for the snow to stop but he looked in horror at the depth of it surrounding the mine. Because of the flat spot from the tailings, it had piled high, before some of it had tumbled down the mountain.

Finally, everything stopped except for the gentle cloud that was settling. The silence was unnerving. Grabbing a shovel, he went to the front of the cave again and called out, "Tracy. Tracy! Can you hear me?"

He thought he heard a soft answer as he pulled on the snowshoes. He crept out onto the snow hoping that it would hold. It seemed to be.

He headed toward the direction that Tracy had been gathering samples, trying to be quiet so that he could hear her. He called out, "Tracy, save your breath but make as much noise as you can. So, I can find you." Often the worst part of an avalanche was lack of air.

After a few moments of breathless fear and him inching forward, he started hearing a tapping noise, she had her rock hammer and her metal collection case with her, and he remembered she'd been filling it up with different specimens to test this weekend. Smart girl.

"I'm coming, keep tapping." The tapping was so quiet he was afraid to breathe. At least it was quiet to him, but he imagined it was loud to her. He followed the sound until he felt he was right on top of her.

"I'm here. I'm here." He couldn't hear what she said back, but she answered him. He needed to hurry, but not panic, he didn't want her to be asphyxiating or getting too cold. She was dressed to work in the cold, but being buried was different, her hands and face and everything would be frozen, especially if she couldn't move, and he needed to see if she was hurt. Rocks and trees had tumbled with the snow, he had to make sure she hadn't been hit by any of them.

He used the shovel first to get down a few feet, after digging for a couple of minutes, he was worried about hitting her with the shovel, so he used his hands to dig, and the shovel to toss away the loosened snow and ice.

Finally, he dug through to where he could see her coat, he grabbed it to let her know he was there, and then started working towards her head. He needed to get her head uncovered. Snow kept falling back into the hole that he dug. But he was getting more out than was falling in so that was a good thing. He ultimately dug his way to her head, she was laying on her stomach, and her hands were wrapped around a tree. That position and the tree had probably helped to maintain a pocket of air.

"Are you all right? Are you hurt?"

She sucked in a deep breath. "I am all right, but one of my legs hurts. It feels maybe twisted, it doesn't feel broken, I got swept off my feet. I managed to crawl up far enough to hold onto this tree and not be swept away."

"That was smart."

"Yeah, when I did that, I laid my collection case next to me. So, I managed to wiggle enough to get to it so I could use it to make noise with my rock hammer."

"Good job. I'll get you out of here as soon as I can." Since he knew how deep he could dig with the shovel until it was just a few inches above her body, he managed to get her uncovered quickly.

"Now you're sure your back doesn't hurt or your neck or anything, right?"

She pushed up. "No, I'm fine."

"Good. Let's get you out of this snow, we don't want any more trouble with it."

She shivered, "Yeah, I don't want to be out here anymore."

Lloyd pulled her out and steadied her as she tried to stand, but one leg was hurting too badly. "I can't, it hurts."

He just picked her up and carried her to the cave. She was a little thing and didn't weigh hardly anything, she had a death grip on her rock hammer and sample case.

"I'm gonna carry you. I don't want to get caught in another snowslide." He felt her shudder and kept talking to get her mind off it. "It's funny we've been out here for days and days and haven't had any trouble. And then today half the mountain comes down. Your trusty rock hammer and collection case were invaluable. Hopefully the collection tubes survived."

"I can always get more samples. I don't know much about avalanches other than to try to get a pocket of air, the tree helped with that."

He chilled at the thought of what might have happened

without that tree to cling to. "Thank God for the tree. I don't know what causes snow to break loose like that. I'll be studying up on that."

She laid her head on his chest and he pulled her in close as he got to the cave entrance. He wanted to simply hold her, but she needed warmth. Inside he turned on the portable heaters. He'd had one light on near where he was working. But he turned on some of the other battery powered lanterns.

Before he could check her leg, he heard the emergency radio squawk. Shit, he figured he'd better let everyone know that they were okay. "Lloyd here."

It was Thomas. "Thank God. Lloyd, are you all right? Is Tracy all right?"

"Yeah. Tracy was buried, but I got her out and we are in the cave. No idea where the snowmobile is, maybe buried, unless it tumbled down the hill. How about the rest of you?"

"We were nearly to cabin two and turned to watch it. It didn't make it this far, so the cabin and the engineer's trailers are fine. When you didn't answer your cell or the radio, I called the National Forest Rangers."

"What did they say?"

"They said unless emergency medical care was needed not to chance leaving right now. They hadn't thought that the snow was unstable. But since we had the snowslide, they didn't want anybody else out in it until they could check it."

"All right, we'll be fine here. We're safe, you guys stay safe too. We have enough food and batteries and everything to last all eight of us a week. The two of us? We could stay here a month. Not that we want to, but we could."

"Yeah, you'll probably need to hunker down at least tonight. We'll be up as soon as we can. I'll talk to Travis about it."

"That's good. I'm gonna check on Tracy, she's got a bit of a sore leg. She thinks it's just sprained."

"I hope that's all it is. Let us know if it's anything she needs medical attention for. We could either try to transport you down or maybe Beau could come up, that would be only a single trip."

That made sense but he hoped it wouldn't be necessary. "I'll let you know."

"We should probably plan check-ins until we can get you out of there, morning and evening?"

"Yeah, we'll see if our phones survived and the cell tower, otherwise we'll use the radio."

"Perfect, good luck."

"Later." Lloyd set down the radio and turned to look at Tracy.

She said, "We're gonna be trapped in here." It wasn't a question, and she didn't look happy about it.

"Yeah, we are."

"I'm glad you're here with me. I don't really like this cave," she shuddered.

"I know, but we'll be fine. Let's make sure your leg is okay and nothing else is hurt. Then we'll work together to get things set up."

"Okay," she said in a whisper.

CHAPTER 7

*H*is phone rang, echoing in the cabin he was renting. A glance at the display showed him who was calling, his asshole brother, Ray, he was going to be pissed.

Buddy pushed answer. "Yeah?"

"Did you really fucking start that avalanche after I specifically told you not to?"

Bossy older brothers were a pain in the ass. "Yeah, I did."

"Did you know you trapped two of them in the mine?"

"Nuh uh, I waited until after everyone left. Or at least they shoulda been gone, I've been watching them for days, they always leave at the same time."

Ray's voice was deadly quiet. "Well, they didn't today, numbskull. Two of them were still there, one got buried and could have died. You're just damn lucky the other one dug her out."

"Her?"

"Yeah, the dark-haired one, I think."

Buddy was sorry to hear it was the little dark-haired cutie. "Damn, she's a mighty fine piece of skirt."

"God dammit. Stop thinking with your dick. You could have killed her and then you would be facing murder charges."

Nag, nag, nag that's all he ever did. "Well, I'm not, I take it she's fine."

"Yes, but we can't go get them out of the damn mine, because now the snow is unstable, which means, idiot, you can't get near the mine, either. You fucked up, brother."

He'd actually figured that out on his own when he'd tried to go down there and slid into a hole, it had taken him time and a lot of cussing to get out of it. Buddy could admit he didn't know much about mountains and snow, coming from Georgia. His bossy brother was learning, after joining up with the Forest Service here in Colorado. It was a big difference from Ray doing the same job in the National Wildlife Refuge swamps. Alligators versus bears or mountain lions, he wasn't all that thrilled that his brother had come with him to take their inheritance back. Ray had insisted, and Buddy had a sneaking suspicion the main reason his big brother had trailed along was to keep an eye on him. He didn't need a damn babysitter.

"Yeah, well we can figure something out."

"You need to stay put until that snow settles," Ray warned.

"Yeah, I got that."

He pushed end and lay back on the bed in their rented space. He needed a better way to get those busy bodies out of the mine. Too bad he'd cleared the bear out last summer; he could have let the bear take care of all those people. Back in the summer he'd figured it would only take a few days to claim their inheritance. But no, they'd spent all damn summer and autumn looking.

A nest of alligators would do it, not that alligators could

43

live in this damn cold, hell, he could barely stand it himself. Buddy fell asleep trying to figure out a new plan.

～

RAY WANTED TO SLAM HIS PHONE, OR HIS HEAD, ON THE steering wheel of his jeep. His brother was a wild card, which is exactly why he'd moved to this frozen wasteland, to keep his eye on Buddy. If he hadn't promised his mother that he'd keep an eye on Buddy, he'd be back in his cozy home, working in his beloved swamps. But no, Buddy had gotten a bug up his butt, shortly after their mother's death, fucking cancer.

Ray could admit he'd loved hearing the stories about the gold mine in Colorado the three brothers had to abandon to return home to fight in the War between the States. Ray enjoyed the stories but had never had the itch to investigate to see if they were true. Or to discover if the brothers had really buried their fortune rather than trying to lug it home during war time. The story went that they'd only brought what they could carry and could easily hide in their meager belongings.

Whether the rest of the story was true or not Ray hadn't known, but Buddy had been convinced. So, Ray had quit his job, closed up his house, and his mother's, and had followed his halfwit brother clear across the country to find this myste-rious and well-hidden treasure. They'd spent the spring last year just trying to find the damn mine. Once they did find it and the tailings, he'd begun to believe maybe it was true.

They'd dug and searched for months and had found noth-ing. They'd tried a little mining themselves at the back of the cave but hadn't been very successful. They didn't know a damn thing about mining, or geology either, for that matter.

Shit, he needed to get back inside; his break was over. He

was on the evening shift this week. He'd expected a quiet night and then that idiot had started an avalanche. It was no longer going to be a quiet night as they geared up for a possible rescue tomorrow. He just hoped that Buddy hadn't left any evidence behind. Dammit he was going to have to volunteer for a double shift to make sure.

CHAPTER 8

*T*racy was trying not to freak out, she'd been scared to death trapped under all that snow, praying Lloyd would find her before she ran out of air or froze. She was so glad she'd not been alone on the mountain, of course she wouldn't have been alone, since they were using two-man snowmobiles for transportation.

But what if she'd been with Brenda? They might have both died. Better not to think about it. She'd been with Lloyd, and he'd picked her up like she weighed nothing. Brenda sure wouldn't have been able to carry her back to the cave. Tracy had to stop thinking about it, she was safe and with someone that knew how to survive in the mountains of Colorado.

He pulled her out of her swirling thoughts. "Do you think we can get the snow pants off without cutting them?"

Cut her snow pants off, was he crazy? "We are not cutting off any of my clothing, especially these snow pants, do you have any idea how much they cost?"

"But we don't want to jar your leg."

"We are not cutting off the snow pants."

Lloyd frowned like he thought she was being irrational. "Where is your leg hurt?"

"My knee. I think I just wrenched it when the snow swept me off my feet. Maybe hyper extended it a bit."

"Okay, well let's try to slide the pants off. I'll take your boots off first."

He was so gentle she barely felt him remove her boots.

"Good, not too much snow got inside, your socks are still dry. Cold but dry."

"Now unfasten the snow pants and I'll see if I can slide them off."

She unfastened her pants and then used her good leg to try to raise up enough to get them over her butt. She fought with them for several minutes before giving up. "I can't get them off my butt. If you can kind of lift me up maybe I can push them off."

"We can try that, sure. If I stand you up on one leg and keep you steady that might work."

He put his hands out to lift her. "No wait, let me unfasten the jeans too, maybe we can get them both over my fat ass."

Lloyd frowned. "You do not have a fat ass."

Tracy laughed at his fierce expression. "I know, it was a joke. But trying to get the pants off with only one leg makes it feel bigger."

Lloyd lifted her onto one foot and kept a firm hold on her while she pushed the snow pants and then her jeans over her butt, leaving them both at mid-thigh and her bottom half in only the thermal underwear and panties.

He sat her down on the camp chair, which was a bit on the chilly side in the two thinner layers, but she would live.

Lloyd knelt at her feet and slowly pulled each layer down her leg and over her feet. He grinned at her in triumph and then seemed to notice she was only in underwear on the

47

bottom half, long thermal underwear, but it still made him blush.

He seemed to look around frantically for a moment and then said, "I-I, um, sh-should get you a blanket so you don't get c-cold."

"I would like one to sit on after we pull the thermal underwear off, this chair is kind of cold."

"The thermal? Oh, can't we just cut them on that one leg, so you can stay covered."

"No, we cannot, I'll need them later."

"We can order you some new ones."

"Lloyd, just try to get them off."

He shrugged like someone being sent off on an onerous chore. "All right. Let me gather the blankets. One for the chair and one for covering you up."

She suspected he was not worried about the cold but about her being scantily clad. "Don't worry, I have granny panties on."

LLOYD DIDN'T KNOW EXACTLY WHAT GRANNY PANTIES WERE, but it didn't matter, whatever she had on was going to affect him, there was no getting around it. This was a clear case of, be careful what you wish for. He'd fantasized about her in a lot less clothes, his hot mouth and hands caressing her curves. But fantasy and real life were two entirely different scenarios.

And this one, with half her clothes off was going to kill him, he was just sure of it. He found two blankets and folded one so it would fit in the chair so she could sit on it, and set the other one nearby to put over her, once they got the thermals off, so he could check her knee. It wouldn't hurt to check the other leg, just to make sure she didn't have any scrapes that needed tending.

Her upper body probably should be checked too. She might have gotten too cold to notice anything other than her wrenched knee. Damn, then she'd have even fewer clothes on to torment him. But he didn't want anything to get infected because he was too much of a chicken to do a thorough job.

"I'm going to pull you up to a standing position again. Just stay there for one second while I put the blanket in the chair and then I'll help keep you steady to pull off the long-johns."

Once she was seated in only her panties, he draped the blanket over her. He'd tried not to ogle her body, she was hurt and needed first aid, but he'd seen it and her panties didn't look like anything a grannie would wear. He had seen what might be a bruise, on her upper thigh and hip.

"I think you have a bruise on your right hip."

"Oh, I forgot all about it, I did feel a rock hit it, but I was too busy trying to cling to the tree to think about it."

Her breath shuddered and she trembled. Was she going into shock? "Hey, let me get you a soda, you might need some sugar after that adrenaline rush."

"I do feel a little shaky."

He grabbed another couple of blankets to wrap around her and found a drink with sugar in it. "Here drink this. Do you want to talk about it? Sometimes it helps."

"No, I'm fine, go on with your triage."

He knelt at her knee to examine it as best he could. It did feel just wrenched and it wasn't very sore as he touched it.

She hiccupped and he looked up to see she was crying. "Hey baby, talk to me."

"Oh, Lloyd I was so scared."

He took her in his arms, and rubbed her back, letting her

49

sob while he muttered soothing nonsense. Lloyd had some tears of his own as he thought back, they'd been damn lucky.

When her tears started to slow, he said, "I know baby. I was terrified myself, so afraid I wouldn't find you."

"But you did. You saved me."

"Because you were smart and hung onto that tree and kept hold of your rock hammer."

"Oh, Lloyd, what if—"

He pulled her in tight and cut her off. "Nope we're not going down the 'what if' path. Fortunately, we were spared all those unpleasant possibilities. You are here, safe in this cave with me. From what I can tell you only have a few bumps and bruises."

She shuddered out a breath. "You're right, I *am* fine, we are both safe."

"I need to finish checking you out, we don't want to miss anything that might cause trouble later. I'm going to wrap up that knee and check the bruise on your hip, then we can check out your upper body and get you back into warm clothes."

As he checked out the rest of her, he managed to keep his mind on the fact she was traumatized and needed medical attention, not some dumbass lusting over her. He found a few more bruises but nothing that needed attention. With her knee wrapped it was much easier to get her re-dressed. The heaters were doing a good job at keeping the chill out of the area they were in.

Lloyd asked, "Are you hungry?"

She shook her head then yawned. "I just want to lay down and rest for a few minutes."

"Good idea, you do that, and we can eat after."

"Would you, um, would you mind holding me while I rest? I could use the comfort and the warmth."

"Of course. Whatever you need." It might test the strength

of his willpower, but he would do whatever he could, whatever she asked.

He made a nice thick bed of all the sleeping bags piled on top of each other, helped her down onto it, then pulled the blankets up over the top of them. He pulled the heaters in close and turned the lights down. She snuggled into his arms and promptly fell asleep. He dozed a bit, but her soft warm body and scent kept him on edge.

He tried to keep his mind on the practicalities of their situation, so it didn't go off on another tangent, one he should steer clear of. He'd not found any head injuries but decided he shouldn't let her sleep too long, just in case. An hour would be fine, probably, he'd wake her in a bit so they could eat before they went to bed for the night.

He'd also need to figure out what they should eat, they'd brought emergency rations and also some canned food. He couldn't start a fire in the cave to heat things up unless it was right near the exit for ventilation. Even that was iffy, with so much snow dumped over them he decided the emergency rations would have to do, at least for tonight. He might be able to dig out enough snow at the mouth of the cave to use a cookstove, but that would be best done in the morning, in the daylight. By morning coffee would probably be a priority, for both of them.

When Tracy woke, she snuggled in closer to him, which had his body reacting. He didn't want her to notice so he gave her a squeeze and then sat up. "I'm getting kind of hungry, are you?"

She sighed and sat up. "I could eat, but I liked cuddling with you better."

He couldn't admit to her that he'd enjoyed her being in his arms a little too much, so he muttered, "Thanks. I, um, like holding you, too."

"Right."

Now he'd hurt her feelings, dammit. "No, I do, it's just, well I like it a little too much."

"You jumped up as soon as I woke up because you like holding me too much? Just what in the hell does that mean?"

All right, pissed was better than hurt, but still not good. He still didn't know what to say, so he got busy making them some dinner. He found canned fruit to go with the rations that would self-heat. There was plenty of bottled water, juice, and soda. The whole time Tracy was sitting on their temporary bed frowning.

He started putting the food on one of the coolers when she giggled. He'd never heard that particular sound come out of her so with a raised eyebrow he asked, "What's so amusing."

She patted the blanket next to her, so he sat. She leaned on him, her head on his shoulder, "So if you like it too much does that mean your body reacts to mine?"

Fuck, now he was in for it. "Let's just eat."

"No. Tell me the truth, Lloyd."

Shit, why hadn't he kept his trap shut, and why did she have to be so smart, and beautiful? With his own sigh, he gave a tiny nod which she obviously felt. She pulled back and grinned up at him. "Perfect, I've been trying to figure out how to convince you that we should become more than friends."

His voice squeaked, "More," he cleared his throat. "More than friends?"

"Yes, as in lovers. I'll be here another five or six months. Plenty of time to enjoy each other. Don't you think?"

Think? She wanted him to think? When all the blood had rushed out of his head and his heart was pounding so hard, he could barely hear. He couldn't remember his own name, let alone think. But she was waiting for an answer.

He managed a nod and a grunt. That seemed to be good enough because she flew at him, grabbed him by the ears and put her hot mouth on his. All he could do was hang on for the ride.

Dear God, the woman could kiss. When she'd sucked all thought and ability to function out of his body she sat back, patted him on the arm and said, "Eat your dinner, you're going to need your strength."

He just sat there dumbfounded and had no idea what the word 'eat' even meant. She giggled at him again and handed him his fork after spearing a piece of meat. "It goes in your mouth, and you chew it."

He managed not to choke on his food and as his blood cooled his thoughts and reasoning returned. Which was a good thing, except for the fact they needed to talk about why her idea of the two of them becoming lovers was a bad idea. She was not going to like that.

He made a list of the reasons it was a bad idea in his head while they ate their dinner in silence. When they were finished eating, he picked up the trash and put it all in a sealed container, one that would not attract wild animals.

Moving one of the chairs over to where she sat on the cobbled together bed, he sat down facing her. "We need to talk."

She sighed, "I just knew you were going to say that."

"Look I find you wildly attractive, but I don't think going to bed with each other is a good idea."

Tracy rolled her eyes at him and folded her arms across her chest. "Fine, tell me all your excuses."

"They are not excuses. I'm too old for you, I'm not smart enough, we live and work in different worlds. I'm just a cowhand and you're going to have a doctorate degree. It's just not a good idea."

She pointed at him. "First, age is just a number and you're not that much older, less than ten years. Second, you are damn smart, you simply have a learning disability. Third, we're going to be in the same world for six months, so it would work just fine."

"But…"

"No, you stop right there. It's not like I'm looking for a husband. I'm not planning to slide you into the position of my forever man." Her voice broke a little on the word forever, but she steeled herself and said, "It's just sex Lloyd, for a season. I just want to enjoy you while I can, temporarily. Is that so bad?"

That hitch in her voice hurt his heart, she'd never had a forever family, only temporary ones, and the idea of being her temporary lover sounded, just sad.

He went down on the blanket next to her and drew her into his arms. "No, baby, that's not bad at all." Sad as fuck, but not bad.

CHAPTER 9

*T*racy didn't want a pity fuck, but since she'd spewed all that crap, how could she be sure? She laid her head on his shoulder as his arms came around her. "I want to have sex with you, but only if you want to. I don't want to be a pity screw."

He laughed, but it was strained. "Tracy there is nothing I would like better than to make love to you, I just don't want you to get hurt."

She turned her head and kissed his neck, she felt him shudder and decided that no, this wouldn't be a pity fuck, the guy was into her.

Lloyd drew her gently down to lie on the stack of sleeping bags, he rolled toward her and gently kissed her mouth. Tingles spread from his lips throughout her body. She gasped and opened her mouth, and his tongue stole inside. The kiss became hotter when she brushed her tongue to his. He moaned in her mouth and his lips started to devour.

Tracy held on to his shoulders, letting the sensations run amok in her bloodstream. He kissed her until she was pliant and aroused. She'd never had a man take such a long time to kiss her, just kiss. It was a wonderful feeling, but she wanted more.

She pulled at the bottom of his shirt, she wanted to get her hands on all that warm flesh. She got one shirt pulled out of his pants and out of the way, while he continued with the long drugging kisses. She sighed when her hands hit the thermal underwear.

"Lloyd, I need skin, can you stop kissing for just a sec., and help me?"

He kissed her on the nose and rose up on his knees. Tossing the flannel shirt and the thermal top to the side he grinned at her. "Better?"

"Much, now get back down here."

"Yes ma'am." His mouth was back on hers in a flash and now she had all that nice warm skin to explore. She felt his muscles jump as she caressed him, but he didn't move from his exploration of her mouth. His hand stayed in her hair or on her shoulders, not venturing forth to where she wanted them.

She started to unbutton her own flannel shirt, not only did she want his skin next to hers, but she was getting hot. The man was a furnace and she had on two layers of warm clothes. After a few moments he noticed what she was doing and drew back, which gave her more room with the pesky buttons.

His voice was gruff when he said, "I'm not sure that's a good idea, Tracy darlin'"

She frowned at him. "I'm not making love to you in my clothes and if I don't' get some of these layers off I am going to combust. You're like my own personal heater."

"Your cheeks *are* a little flushed."

"From heatstroke, now help me get these off."

With a chuckle his hands joined hers. He helped her sit

once the shirt was unbuttoned and he pulled it off to join his, then he helped her remove the thermal top. She unhooked her bra and sent it flying. Leaving her fully clothed on the bottom, which confused her a little, but she decided he needed to take things slowly and pulled him back down on top of her, so their bare chests met. The skin on skin gave her exquisite feelings.

He went back to kissing and holding on to her shoulders. She allowed it for a bit since the man could really kiss, but after a while she took one hand and led it down to her breast. He groaned as his fingers closed around the soft mound and she felt exactly the same way.

He continued the kisses, but they grew hotter and deeper as his hands explored her breasts. Now they were getting somewhere. Slowly, so darn slowly. The man was part snail, at least in the bedroom.

"Lloyd, I love the kisses, but do you think we could move along to more sexy stuff and maybe lose the rest of our clothes?"

"I don't have any protection with me."

"I'm clean. I haven't been with anyone for a long time. And I had a physical recently where they checked for stuff, all negative. Plus, I'm on long term birth control. So, I'm willing to go commando, if you're clean too."

He chuckled. "I never thought of that word in quite that way, but I'm clean too."

"Goody, so now can we move this party along? Um, if you want to, that is."

"I'm a little worried about hurting your knee, too."

She felt so cared for, with a kiss on his chin she said, "I'll just lie still and let you do all the work."

His grin was lopsided. "I can do that. I would be happy to do all the work, in fact."

"Until next time when my knee is better, and then there are no promises."

~

LLOYD DIDN'T KNOW WHAT TO THINK ABOUT THE NEXT TIME comment. It sounded to him like the woman was planning to keep up the lovemaking beyond their time in the mine. He knew the Kiplings had told Thomas he was welcome in the big house and in Brenda's bed, but it felt a little awkward to him.

Tracy's hands went to his belt, and he decided to think about later, well, later. He had a hot and needy woman in his arms, and he'd promised her to do all the work so she wouldn't injure her knee, which meant he needed to get after it.

He rose up and went to work on her jeans and then the thermal underwear, they'd been down this road earlier today but not quite for this purpose, so if he fumbled a bit with removing her clothes no one could blame him. The woman was gorgeous with her hourglass figure.

He pulled the clothes away until she only had on her blue panties. God, she was amazing and wanted to share herself with him. How in the hell did he get so lucky? She pushed at her panties, and he got the hint and carefully removed them, now she was fully naked except for the ace bandage on her knee. He wanted to worship every inch, slowly, for hours, maybe days.

Tracy had other ideas and went back to tugging at his belt. So, he stripped himself of his clothes. Before he joined her on their makeshift bed, he turned most of the lanterns down and some of the heaters also, it was plenty warm in the cave, and he didn't want to run out of juice. Once his chores were finished, and he joined her back on the bed, he had to worship that body for a few minutes. He wasn't going to get a long time because as soon as he got near, she took his rod in her hand and squeezed it gently, running those fingers up and down, her thumb moving across the head.

He groaned. "Tracy, if you don't stop that, this is going to be over way too soon."

She giggled and let go. "All right if you insist, at least for now. But if you don't fill me I'll have no choice about touching."

He moved over in between her legs. "I was going to explore your beautiful body, but I can be obedient."

"Good we can both explore next time. But right now, I want the invasion, the filling, give me that cock before I explode." Then she took him in hand and guided him to where she wanted him.

He slid into her hot, wet warmth, and felt her flesh close around him. It was the first time he'd ever had unprotected sex and he was shocked by the difference in sensations, everything was sharper, more intense. He gritted his teeth, to keep from coming, before he pleasured her. His job was to give her the first orgasm and he was not going to shortchange her.

She squeezed him with her inner muscles, his signal to start moving.

As he filled her over and over again, his mouth devoured hers, he just couldn't get enough of that warm mouth, she kissed like a goddess. Her tongue tangling with his, giving him little nips and then soothing the tiny ache with her tongue. His hands covered her breasts, while using his elbows to keep from squishing her.

She wrapped her good leg around his waist leaving the other stretched out on the pile of sleeping bags. It opened up a small gap where he could reach in and tease her clit, she groaned with the pressure. As she got closer to climax, her movements became frantic, so he sped up to accommodate her.

Tracy went off like a bottle rocket, squeezing his ass with one hand and nearly pulling out all his hair with the other. He hardly noticed as his orgasm claimed him in an avalanche of pleasure. He just barely managed to get back on his elbows, so he didn't mash her into the hard floor of the cave.

The leg around his waist slid off as she turned boneless, Lloyd was pleased he'd put her in that state. He rolled to his side and pulled the blankets up over the top of their cooling bodies.

Tracy snuggled into his chest and muttered, "Thanks, just what the doctor ordered."

He grinned as he held her close and shut his eyes against the dim light he'd left burning in the mine.

They'd woken several times in the night to make love again. Once she'd gotten started, Lloyd found the woman insatiable. He did his best to satisfy her, and he did for a few hours, but then she'd wake up raring to go again. Not that he was complaining, but he'd never been with a woman that liked sex as much as Tracy did.

He tried not to worry about the sex being a coping mechanism for her past. Lloyd wasn't completely successful at that, and his heart ached for the beautiful woman in his arms.

CHAPTER 10

*L*loyd managed to free himself from Tracy. He wanted to make their living conditions a little better. He dressed quietly and took the shovel out so he could secure a place where they could cook, and a few other necessities. He wanted to see if the snowmobile was still nearby or if it had been pushed down the hill.

As he worked clearing snow away from the mouth of the cave, he thought about Tracy and his revelations in the night as he'd held her close. He knew he was already half in love with her, maybe more than half, but theirs was a short-term relationship. He'd miss her when she left to go back to school.

When he'd cleared enough snow, not to disturb her when he called the ranch, he did so. Thomas answered on the first ring. "Are you guys all right?"

"We are, since we'd brought up enough supplies for all of us, we've been very cozy. I'm out making a place to cook, and I haven't quite made it over to see if the snowmobile is still here."

"Good, don't venture too far, we don't know how stable the snow is around you yet."

Lloyd asked, "Did you hear from the Forest Service today?"

"Yeah, they checked along the road and there wasn't a slide anywhere else. So, they looked around above the mine and didn't think the snowslide looked natural."

"What?"

"Yeah, they think it was man-made, so keep your wits about you and one of the rifles close by. Just in case."

"Well shit. I left Tracy sleeping in the cave."

"She should be fine. Even if some dumbass did start the avalanche, he's unlikely to want to traverse the loose snow. I'll get back to you when I hear back from them. They were talking about climbing down from the road with ropes and stuff to get you out."

"Yeah, keep me informed."

"Will do. How is Tracy's knee?"

"Just sprained. It isn't giving her too much trouble." The entertainment during the night had solidified that. He still wanted to check it, when she woke up.

"Good. I don't think you'll be there any longer than maybe one more day."

Lloyd glanced to the mouth of the cave and saw Tracy wrapped in a blanket. "Great, my phone is fine. I'm not sure about Tracy's but we've got mine and the radio and some power banks."

"Brenda is probably going to want to talk to Tracy."

"Anytime."

Pushing end and sliding his cell phone into his pocket, Lloyd walked over to the mouth of the cave where Tracy was standing just inside of it wrapped in a blanket. He thought maybe only a blanket, which if circumstances were different, he'd take her right back to that palette, but he figured it was time to get dressed. "What are you doing here? You don't even have shoes on."

"You left me?"

"No, I didn't leave you. But I did shovel out an area where we could put the Coleman stove and get some coffee on. I figured both of us would want that, more than air, about now."

She laughed. "Yeah, I'm kind of feeling that way. I see that other path. What's that for?"

"You know, like, using the facilities."

"Oh, I'm gonna need to do that pretty quick."

"Well, let me check your knee first, and we'll get it rewrapped if it needs to be. I'll help you get dressed so you can go off into the bushes, so to speak."

"Or snowbank."

"Whatever."

She laughed, and they went inside where she kept the blanket wrapped around her and sat in the camp chair.

He carefully unwrapped her knee. "How's it feeling?"

"It feels fine. I don't know that it even needs to be wrapped anymore."

"Well, since I think what you did was hyper-extend it, I think we'll leave it wrapped. At least another day."

"Okay."

"Hyperextensions can flare up if you're not careful with them."

"Okay."

He looked at her knee and moved it all around and she didn't seem to have any pain. So, he rewrapped it and helped her get her thermal underwear on over some clean panties that she had in her pack and then her jeans. She pulled her sports bra on, the thermal top, and flannel shirt.

63

He helped her put her boots on over some nice thick socks and decided that was good. She wouldn't want her snow pants on. In fact, he wondered if he should have left the thermals off, but they'd all been using the facilities with their snow gear on for a couple of days, so she probably had it down.

She stood and went to the front of the cave.

"Do you need any help?"

"No, I'll be fine." She said and went off down the path that he'd made.

While she did that, he went back out and kept digging towards where the snowmobile should be. When he got within two feet of where it should be he breathed a sigh of relief when he saw the outline of it and knew that it was only buried, not pushed down the hill. After they had some breakfast, he'd come back out to get it out from underneath the snow.

But right now, he figured the coffee would be about done and he could start some breakfast foods. They'd brought up a carton of fake eggs. Well, not fake eggs, exactly. But not in their shells either. And they had some bacon and even some bread. He took the coffee pot and put it on the back corner where it would stay warm and got out a pan, throwing some bacon in, he let that cook while he got a couple of mugs for coffee. When he got back out with the coffee mugs and a plate, Tracy was back and grabbed one of the coffee cups out of his hand, she poured herself a cup of coffee.

"There might be cream or sugar in there." He pointed toward the cave.

"Nope. Black is fine. I don't think those percolators make coffee quite as strong as modern-day appliances, do you?"

"No, I don't think so. Although I did put a fair amount of coffee beans in there. But they only hold so much."

Tracy blew on her coffee and took a tiny sip. "Ah, perfect."

He grinned at her as he put the bacon onto the plate and then poured in the eggs.

"That bacon looks yummy."

"Yeah, but you need to let it cool first, shouldn't take long out here."

"No probably not. Did you find the snowmobile?" she asked.

"I did in fact, and I talked to Thomas."

"Is that who you were talking to when I came out?"

He rubbed one hand on the back of his neck, he dreaded telling her this part. "Yes. The Forest Service doesn't think it was a natural avalanche. So, they're investigating before they determine what should be done. Thomas thought we might need to stay here one more day. But if they decide the snow is stable enough, they might come get us earlier, they're talking about using ropes to get down to us so that if the snow starts to slip, they'll be tied up above."

TRACY SHUDDERED AT THE THOUGHT THAT SOMEONE HAD deliberately tried to bury them in an avalanche. "Why would someone try and kill us in an avalanche?"

"I've been thinking on that," Lloyd said. "I'm not sure they were. We were here later than normal. And it could be that they were just trying to bury the mine so we couldn't get to it so easily."

"And we would just leave it like that for the winter?"

He shrugged. "I don't know the way people think."

"Well, I don't think if someone did do it, that they're thinking very clearly or very intelligently."

"I couldn't agree more." He slid the eggs onto the plate and turned off the Coleman stove. "We've got bread inside and if you want toast, I can make some."

"No this is good. Eggs and bacon are enough. And coffee. Lots of coffee."

He carried the plate of food inside and she carried the coffee pot. He divided the food onto two plates, and they sat in camp chairs to eat.

Tracy didn't think she'd ever had breakfast that tasted so good and told Lloyd that.

"Eating outdoors over a campfire or Coleman stove always seems to taste better. Plus, what we had for dinner last night wasn't exactly stellar."

She laughed. "That's true, but it did fill the belly."

"Yes, it did."

"So, if we have to stay up here for lunch what do we have?"

"Well, like I said, we have bread, since we've only been set up here a week, it should still be good. We'll bring new bread up in a few days, providing we can get back up at all. We've got canned chicken, and canned tuna, all kinds of chips, because they don't go bad, cookies and various granola snacks. So, we're not going to starve." He was so cute trying to reassure her.

"Not at all. We'll be fine. Providing we don't get out of here today. I really want to get back to the house. But at the same time, I kind of enjoy the intimacy that we have here."

He took her hand and squeezed. "I'll talk to Meg or Travis and let them know that our relationship has changed, and I'll be at the house more in the evening."

Her quick bright smile seemed to dazzle him. "Good. So, to keep me distracted, tell me about your time at the gold mine when you were a kid, did you like it?"

"No, I was too ticked off about having to leave school and friends. I hated mining. My father got a bug up his butt about it when I hit fourth grade and pulled me out of school, saying we were moving. I hadn't wanted to go, I'd finally found a teacher who was helping me, and had wanted to stay in school, I had trouble reading and I wanted extra help to over-come it. My fourth-grade teacher was willing to put in the extra time with me."

"Oh man, that sucks."

"Yeah, and I'd also wanted to play baseball in the summer and soccer in the spring. But no, I had to go with my dad to 'strike it rich' at a fricken gold mine, that they'd never gotten much of a profit from. So, a big fat waste of time and I didn't find another teacher to help."

Her heart hurt for the little boy with a reading disability. "So much might have been different for you if that hadn't happened."

"Yeah, but when you got out of that Range Rover and stretched, I changed my mind and decided maybe being assigned to your team would be good. Finally, something good to come from my father's wild hair."

She laughed as he tried to lighten the discussion. "Well, I can admit that I'd wanted you to stay that first day when you showed me to my room."

"You did?"

"Oh yeah. You were a good-looking guy, tall, well built. Filled your wranglers very well, and your dark hair and bright blue eyes, were a winning combination. You talked about the ranch, and I knew I asked kind of stupid questions when you chuckled."

"Sorry about that. I'd been nervous about looking like a dumb cowboy and was blathering on."

She shook her head. "But you didn't shame me or make

me feel foolish. You just answered my questions. So, I learned more about what was going on. I have to admit I still didn't know what a lot of what you said meant. You talked about different kinds of cattle and horses, and how much acreage the ranch had."

She looked around as if making sure no one was listening, then whispered, "I had to look up what an acre was."

He laughed. "I should have known, city girl that you were."

"Hey, I'd been to the country. Not on anything as large as this seemed to be. Just an outdoor camp."

She stopped speaking abruptly, as tears choked her.

"Hey, what's wrong?"

"It doesn't matter."

"Tell me," he said, as he took her hand.

"The only time I'd been out in the country was when the foster family I was with had wanted to get rid of me for a few days. They signed me up for outdoor camp, and then, they w-went to Disneyland. They said they couldn't afford one more kid." She'd yearned to go with them, but she wasn't really part of the family and never had been, not since the day her parents died. But she'd lived through it.

Lloyd swore. "That was just cruel."

"I've still never been." Her voice was so small, like the child she'd been.

"I'll take you. The very next time you have a week free, we'll go."

"Thanks, but my time is going to be packed until I grad-uate a year from now."

"Fine, it will be your graduation gift from me."

She smiled because he wanted her to, but she knew in her heart he wouldn't be around that long.

The only one that had stayed by her side was Brenda.

She'd met Brenda in her first year in school. With Brenda's toxic parents, they'd spent the vacations together. On summer vacations they went out to see the world. Their joint love of geology and the mineral sciences had given them plenty of places to explore.

They didn't stay in five-star hotels, even though Brenda had wanted to a few times. Tracy had shown her the way of youth hostels and campgrounds. They stayed on the outskirts of big cities, wherever they could. On short vacations like Christmas or spring break they explored the surrounding states.

They stayed in the US, there were plenty of geological wonders, they could explore in North America. They were working their way through the National Parks. That would change now that Brenda was graduating, but she and Brenda'd had a few wonderful years, to hold tight in her heart and memories.

CHAPTER 11

*T*racy finally got her phone out from where she had stored it in her snowsuit. The battery was down to two percent, other than that she didn't see any damage. Lloyd found a charger and she plugged it in. She wouldn't know if it had internal problems until it got some juice, she would have to be patient.

She knew Brenda would be worried and she wanted to use her own phone to call if at all possible. It was a fast-charging power bank so she would have enough juice to call after a few minutes charging.

"Can you text Thomas and let him know I'll call Brenda as soon as my phone charges?"

"Sure, I'm glad, it looks like your phone made it through the avalanche."

"Me too. I won't know for sure until I can try it out, but it seems all right, those heavy-duty cases are worth their weight in gold."

"Yeah, we all have them, occasionally if a phone hits just right or a cow steps on it, then they can't compete with that."

Tracy laughed at the picture in her head, of a cow

standing on a phone. "One of these days I want to go out and see the cows."

Lloyd grinned at her. "We can do that on one of the weekends. When you aren't doing the engineering work and don't have too many class assignments. It might be more fun if we wait until it warms up some."

"Spring break is the last week of March."

He touched the tip of her nose in a teasing gesture. "We could still have three feet of snow then, but we can keep it in mind. You might enjoy watching a birth."

The thought of that kind of turned her stomach, all the blood and amniotic fluid, not her idea of fun. Seeing calves after they were born would be enjoyable, however. She didn't quite know what to say so she asked, "Will you need to help on the ranch during the height of the birthing time?"

"Maybe. If Travis needs me or Thomas, he'll check with your boss first. It can get crazy busy, but he tried to hire a couple more townies to help out this year, knowing we might be busy up here at the mine."

"Townies?"

"Temp workers that live in town and help out on several different ranches. Some of them live over in Granby and can circulate easier."

"Oh, I had no idea." She knew so little about ranching, it was pathetic. Maybe Lloyd could teach her some more. "Teach me about ranching while we wait for my phone to charge."

LLOYD DIDN'T KNOW WHAT SHE WANTED TO LEARN BUT HE could start telling her all about the different cattle that they had, and how many horses, and how many acres of ground they had and what they were used for, grazing, planting, housing, all the things. He just kept running his mouth to keep her entertained.

She asked intelligent questions, mostly, there were a few questions that clearly told him, she'd never been in a real rural setting. She was clearly a city girl, a beautiful, smart city girl, not for him.

He was a cowboy. A barely educated cowboy who worked on a ranch in the mountains and had to have another cowboy with him at all times to help him with his letters, and his numbers. She knew about his issues and didn't seem to let that bother her, but it bothered him. She'd never actually seen him when he needed to use numbers and letters, so she'd never seen the full extent of his issues, and that was just fine with him.

After they'd talked for a while, her phone beeped with an incoming text. She plucked it up, it's from Brenda. I think I've got enough power for a chat. "You don't mind if I call her, do you?'

'Not at all, in fact, I'm going to take a short walk, give Thomas a call, and then see if I can rustle us up some lunch, so take your time."

He noticed relief cover her face as he got up to leave, and he wondered what she wanted to share with her bestie. He was glad she'd be occupied; he wanted some time to see what Thomas had heard from the Forest Service guys without worrying Tracy.

Lloyd wasn't so much worried about being rescued, but he was concerned about some crazy out there causing trouble. They did have one firearm with them for wild animals. He'd not gotten it out yet, but wondered if he should. He didn't want to be blindsided and naïve. He'd talk to Thomas and then decide.

He grabbed his phone and walked out into the bright sunshine, after the dimness of the cave it took his eyes a minute to adjust. The snow sparkled, it was easily waist high from the avalanche and even higher than that in places. He couldn't fathom someone deliberately causing that kind of trouble.

He walked down the path he'd cleared and then called Thomas.

Thomas answered, "Hey, how's it going. I thought you might call since Brenda wouldn't wait one moment longer before trying Tracy's phone."

"Yeah, it was out of power, but seems to be fine otherwise. Tracy was just waiting until it charged long enough to call. Those girls are inseparable. So, tell me what you've heard."

"It's not good news. The Forest Service thinks the snow is too unstable to risk coming after you, at least today. They want to give the sun and warmer temps some time to let the snow settle."

"Including me trying to get the snowmobile dug out and maybe making a snow ramp to get it on top."

"Yeah, they said there can be pockets of air or shrubs or trees that can look stable, but they really aren't. They are advising you to stay put for now."

Lloyd sighed; he knew Tracy wouldn't be happy about another night in the mine. "Do they still think it was deliberate?"

"Oh, yeah, in fact they are more certain of it now than they were this morning."

"Do you think we should be worried about someone trying to gain access to the mine?"

Lloyd heard the hesitation loud and clear. "I don't want to be an alarmist, but I'd keep the rifle handy, if I were you."

"If what the Forest Service is saying is true, he'd be a damn fool to try."

"He was a damn fool to start the snow slide in the first place, so I don't know that he's going to get smarter, or try to take advantage of the fact he thinks the mine is empty. At least I hope that's what he thinks."

"Yeah, that was my sense too, he waited until damn near dark before setting it off, probably thought we'd be long gone, and would have been, normally."

Thomas said, "I wonder if he's been watching us."

"Hmm, never thought of that, but it would make sense. It's pretty damn cold out to just sit and watch a bunch of us. The weather is so unpredictable up here."

"He may not know that; he might be from somewhere that early March is turning into spring."

Lloyd chuckled at the thought. "Could be, it sure as hell isn't spring-like this year. Some years when we're having no snowfall it can be, but not this year."

Thomas said, "Last year was dry, and it would have been about the right time to cause us trouble."

"Yeah, spring and right on through early summer, with the snow runoff and those big thunderstorms we had."

"True, those torrential rains might have done it. Well, keep the rifle handy and the woman in sight, hunker down for another night and keep in touch."

"Will do. Let us know if there is anything we need to know."

Thomas said, "Of course. Be careful up there."

Lloyd slid his phone back in his pocket and headed back toward the cave, he didn't want to leave Tracy for too long, and he needed to get the rifle on standby. He hoped he wouldn't need it. Maybe the dumbass had crawled back in his hole.

~

TRACY NEARLY CRIED IN RELIEF WHEN LLOYD WALKED BACK into the cave. Her conversation with Brenda had scared the crap out of her.

Tracy had first reassured Brenda, that she was fine physically, that there was no real problem other than maybe hyperextending her knee a little bit. Then they got to giggling about the fact that she and Lloyd were now lovers. That lasted more than a few minutes, and Tracy was really glad that Lloyd had gone off on his own, so that she and Brenda could talk about it.

After that, Brenda had scared the crap out of her!

Brenda reported that after Thomas had spoken to the Forest Service, he'd gotten agitated about the fact that Lloyd and Tracy were going to have to spend one more night in the cave. That someone had definitely deliberately started the avalanche.

Apparently, Thomas had speculated that maybe the guy had been watching them for a few days or longer and had gotten their schedule down. At least enough to assume he could start the avalanche after they were gone for the day and then would have the place to himself. Which meant he could show up at any time, provided he didn't sink into the unstable snow.

Once Brenda had told her all that, Tracy felt nervous about staying in the mine by herself. What if the guy came, didn't fall into a hole in the snow, but managed to come down the mountain and into the cave? What would she do?

After hanging up from talking to Brenda, she decided her best weapon was her rock hammer, so she got it and held it in her lap. She could whack somebody with that. If she had to. The pointy end could do some damage.

While she waited for Lloyd to get back, she held the rock hammer, softly humming the Beatles song, Maxwell's Silver Hammer. As soon as Lloyd got back, she rushed over to him. "Brenda said we need to be prepared in case someone comes."

"Yeah, I'm gonna get the rifle and make sure it's loaded. Hopefully, I won't have to use it."

She waved her rock hammer in the air. "I've got my trusty rock hammer, just in case."

"That's a good idea. I've got one too. We'll keep those beside us, as well. But in truth, that guy would be an idiot to try and come down that loose snow. Did Brenda tell you that we're gonna need to spend another night here?"

"Yeah. She said the Forest guys want to let the snow settle or something like that."

Lloyd nodded. "With the warmer temperatures and the sun out, it should settle pretty quickly. We've got enough food and everything to keep us set up nicely for a while. But maybe we should stay together if we go outside the cave."

Tracy shuddered, but then agreed. "Yeah, probably, two against one and all that."

After a moment's hesitation she asked. "Do you think there's more than one?"

"Naw, I can't imagine more than one person thinking starting a snow slide would be a good idea."

She could tell her smile was shaky, but it was the best she could manage.

CHAPTER 12

*L*loyd did his best to keep Tracy's spirits up, but he was worried too, so it wasn't easy. Both of them were nervous about some lunatic showing up at any moment, or when least expected. They had their rock hammers within easy reach and the rifle close by.

They made lunch together, and while they tried to act normal and carry on a conversation, they both kept shooting nervous looks all around, searching for possible trouble. They spoke in near whispers and Lloyd had the thought that maybe they should be loud and noisy so if the guy did come close, he might hear they were in residence and go away. It was a good thought, but he couldn't bring himself to do it.

"But if we're noisy then we can't listen for him," Tracy said after he told her of his idea.

And there it was in a nutshell. They didn't want to be surprised by the guy. Lloyd took her hand and rubbed his thumb across her knuckles. "Yeah, that's exactly it. I'm thinking we're going to want to stay dressed tonight, just in case."

Her shoulders slumped. "I know, I'd feel nervous otherwise, even though he would have to be completely insane to try to navigate that snow in the dark."

"Agreed, but still…"

"I just want to get off this mountain and back to my nice cozy room. Last night was amazing, I'd love to repeat it tonight." She looked nervously around, then shrugged. "Not happening."

"Nope, we can do a repeat when we get back to your nice cozy room."

"Promise?"

"Absolutely."

They spent an uneasy afternoon and evening waiting for something to happen, the fact that nothing did happen, almost made it worse, at least in Lloyd's mind. Something to actually do would have been better than the constant tension.

It was growing dark outside as the sun set. "I hate this waiting and wondering," Tracy said.

"Yeah, it's hard on the nerves, I'm going to dig out the snowmobile tomorrow and see if I can make a ramp for it to get on top of the snow. I don't want to just sit here another day. We leave tomorrow, one way or another, unless someone presents me with some hard evidence of why we shouldn't go."

Tracy nodded slowly. "I think I'd rather take my chances with Mother Nature than sit here waiting for some crazy guy to show up."

"Would it make you feel better tonight if I stand watch?"

"No, once it gets dark, I think we'll be safe. Maybe not enough to get undressed, but enough to sleep."

Lloyd said, "We could rig up some kind of noise maker, once we're ready to sleep. We could string it across the cave entrance."

"That might be nice. It would give us some warning."

"Exactly."

Tracy's smile was much more normal than it had been all day. "That's a great idea. We have pans and stuff that would make noise."

Planning a booby trap gave them something to focus on besides their fear. Lloyd cooked them dinner while Tracy kept finding things to tie together to make noise. Dinner was much more relaxed than lunch had been.

When they were ready for bed, they laughed about their booby trap which calmed them enough to sleep. Lloyd set his phone to wake him up at first light, he wanted to call Thomas early, because he was determined to get them back to the ranch.

TRACY WOKE WHEN LLOYD'S PHONE WENT OFF, THE TWO OF them were wrapped together, fully clothed but it still felt intimate, maybe more intimate than when they'd slept naked. This closeness was not after a night of sex, this was just because of affection.

She snuggled in and he kissed her on the forehead after turning off the alarm on his phone.

"This is nice," his growly morning voice skittered along her nerves.

"I was thinking the same thing. We didn't have anyone disturb our early warning system."

"Not complaining. How did you sleep?"

"Like a baby, all warm and snuggled next to you, even in my clothes I slept fine."

He pulled her in tight and then let her go. "I slept fine too, but I am getting us out of here today, whether the Forest Service people agree or not."

"Good. I want a shower, clean clothes, and my bed."

"Right there with you. So do you want to whip us up some coffee and breakfast, while I go see if I can unearth the snowmobile?"

"I could do that. Are you going to call Thomas?" she asked.

"Yeah, but I'll give him an hour, and time to contact the Rangers. I want to have a solid start on getting the snowmobile out before I talk to him."

"All right, I'll make coffee and bring it over to where we parked the snowmobile. Then I'll start breakfast."

"Great plan. Coffee is the first priority."

"I'll keep my rock hammer handy. You take the rifle."

"I will, but I'm thinking he's smart enough to stay away."

Tracy hoped Lloyd was correct in his assumption, but she wasn't letting her guard down. Not for one minute.

She managed to get the coffee and the Coleman stove lit. What she didn't know and hadn't asked was how she was supposed to know when the coffee was ready. She finally decided she'd just pour a little into a cup every so often until it was the right color.

When it seemed right, she filled two travel mugs, they'd washed out yesterday and took them with her to find Lloyd. She decided the coffee was not the best she'd ever tasted but the caffeine was appreciated.

He had the snowmobile mostly uncovered when she found him, and he'd taken off some of his winter gear. His hair was damp with sweat. He gulped down the coffee like a starving man.

"It's got some grounds in it," she said sheepishly.

"Just some fiber."

Tracy pointed at the snowmobile. "You've got it uncovered."

"Almost, I have to clear the exhaust and around the belt before I start it up."

"It gives me hope to see it. I don't feel so stranded."

Lloyd nodded in agreement. "Yeah. I'm going to finish, and I'll call Thomas while we eat."

"Then I'll go cook so we can get off this mountain."

He kissed her hard and quick, then turned back to work, leaving his cup in the snow next to the rifle and his coat.

She managed to make bacon and eggs, and she even toasted some bread, although it was darker on one side than the other. Once it was all ready, she plated it up and left it on top of the turned-off stove where she hoped it would stay warm. It would only take her a minute to get Lloyd, in fact she was a little surprised he hadn't gotten done by now and come back for breakfast.

When she got to the snowmobile, she didn't see him. His coffee cup was laying on its side next to his coat, but the rifle was gone, the snow where it had been was all scuffled looking. She called out, but there was no answer.

She called out louder as panic rose in her chest. The snow was disturbed heading both uphill and down. She didn't know which way to go or if she should go at all. Grabbing her phone out of her pocket with trembling hands, she selected his name. It started ringing, dammit she heard it coming from his coat.

She called out louder. "Lloyd, where are you?"

She thought she heard a faint voice. Was he trapped in the snow somewhere? Had the bad guy gotten ahold of him? Should she go up or down to look for him? She called out again and heard his voice, louder this time.

It sounded like he said, "I'm coming back."

But what if she was wrong, what if he needed help, she was nearly hysterical when she finally saw him trudging back uphill through the snow. When he got to her, she flung herself into his arms, then pulled back and slugged him in the gut.

"Oof. What was that for?"

"For scaring me half to death." She turned and marched back toward the mine entrance.

He followed. "I was just checking out to see if we can get down the hill."

She whirled around and poked him in the chest. "That was really stupid, what if you'd gotten buried in the snow?"

He held up his hands. "But I didn't."

She was too mad to look at his stupid face, so she turned and kept marching down the path. When she got to the stove, she grabbed his plate and shoved it into his hands. "You could have, and I wouldn't have known where to find you."

Tears filled her eyes and she turned her back on him, stupid man.

His plate clattered back onto the stove, and he pulled her into his arms. "I'm sorry."

She sobbed on his chest. In between sobs she choked out, "You didn't have your phone." Sob. "I didn't know if you went up or down." Sob. "What if the bad guy had you?" Sob. "W-what if you got hurt and buried and I couldn't find you?"

"Oh baby, I'm so sorry I scared you. I just wanted to see if the snow was stable. When I heard you call out, I realized I'd gone farther than I thought."

Her sobs turned to hiccups, and she needed a tissue. She dug one out of a pocket, wiped her tears, blew her nose, and turned toward the stove. "And now our breakfast is cold and nasty."

He picked up his plate, put the eggs on the toast, piled the bacon on top and took a huge bite. After he chewed and swallowed, he said, "Tastes great. Bacon and toast don't need to be warm, and the egg is just filler."

She followed suit and decided it wasn't horrible.

They ate in silence for a few minutes and then her curiosity got the best of her. "So, what did you discover while you were scaring the hell out of me?"

"I think we can get out. I need to call Thomas." He patted his pockets.

"Your phone is in your coat. I heard it ring when I tried to call you."

He grimaced and grabbed his coat. "Not my brightest moment."

She wanted to say something snarky but let him call Thomas instead.

CHAPTER 13

*T*homas answered on the first ring. "Hey, how's it going."

Lloyd said, "Good enough. But we want off this damn mountain. I got the snowmobile uncovered and it started."

"No need, the Forest Service guys should be there in an hour, or so."

With a deep sigh, he sent Tracy a thumbs up. She sat down right in the snow and put her head back onto the rock behind her, shutting her eyes, with relief etched across her face.

"Good, we're getting a little stir crazy up here."

Thomas chuckled. "I can imagine. Well, pack everything back up, you'll be out and back here for lunch."

"Not going to argue about that. Anything else we should know?" He didn't want to mention anything that would worry Tracy, but wanted to be prepared for trouble.

"Nope, no trace of anyone. He probably hightailed it out when his little snow slide was bigger than he planned."

"Cool, well, we'll talk more when we get to the ranch."

He pushed end and slid his phone in his pocket. "Thomas said the Forest guys will be here in an hour or two."

"Thank God."

"We need to get everything cleaned up and stored while we wait. I'll make a list of the food we ate so it can be replenished. We can take the sheets and towels we used with us to put in the washer."

"I'll get started on the bedding, you work on the food and stuff. And we have to put away our alarm system."

He chuckled. "Yeah, we shouldn't need it now."

She grinned but quickly sobered. "It might be worth getting some kind of surveillance up here though."

Lloyd nodded slowly as he thought about her suggestion. Having eyes up here wouldn't be a bad idea. "Yeah, even just a trail camera or two. I'll talk to Travis when we get back about that idea."

"You might ask the Forest people too, since the mine is actually on their property."

"True, funny how the border runs right between the mine and the tailings."

Tracy stood and started folding up the blankets and Lloyd figured that was his cue to get busy. They worked in companionable silence. He stayed alert for signs of the Forest Service or the guy that was causing trouble.

THE LAST SLEEPING BAG WAS ROLLED UP AND STORED UNDER the protective tarp. Tracy had neatly folded the soiled sheets and towels and, at Lloyd's insistence, had put them in his pack. Everything was stored, and clean for the next time. Lloyd had a list of food they needed to replace.

After looking around he nodded and took her hand. "Let's sit by the entrance."

Tracy noticed he brought the rifle with him, and she wondered if it was safe to leave it in the mine. If there was someone poking around, could he use it against them? They sat at the entrance to the cave where they could see the paths he'd made. The day was partly cloudy, so the sun came and went, making the snow sparkle and shine, and then leaving it dull and kind of dirty looking, when the sun went behind a cloud.

"Are you taking the rifle with you or leaving it in the mine?"

"Good question. I was debating that myself. If we were taking the snowmobile, I'd probably take it, but if we have to climb the mountain to get back to the road, I'm not sure I want to carry it."

"Will we need the snowshoes? I'm not very good on them."

"You've gotten a lot better."

She grinned, thinking of her first day on them and how she'd kept falling. Brenda hadn't done much better, and they'd ended up laughing their asses off. The men had tried to be stoic, and encouraging, but she and Brenda had seen the mirth sparkle in their eyes.

"Still, that will be a heck of a hike uphill to try to navigate with them."

"Better to be on top of the snow, than slogging through it."

She supposed he had a point, but she wasn't looking forward to it.

Tracy was relieved when she heard the sound of snowmobiles coming toward them. If that was the sound of their rescue, she'd worried for nothing.

Lloyd stood, the rifle in his arms, ready for trouble. "Stay back, just in case. I'm ninety-nine percent sure it's the Forest Service guys, but I don't want to be wrong and give them you as a target."

With a shiver at his words, she drew back, holding her rock hammer as a weapon. The sound of the engines grew louder, then Lloyd lowered the rifle, and a grin broke out on his face. Tracy peered out of the cave, just in time to see Brenda leap off one of the snowmobiles and come running. The ground was still icy, so even though she slipped some, she made it to Tracy in seconds and head her wrapped in a bear hug.

"You're all right?"

Tracy laughed, though tears were clogging her throat. "I will be if you don't crush all the air out of me. I didn't expect you to come with them."

"Thomas said he was going, and I wasn't about to be left behind. We have a truck on the upper road. So, we just have to get us all up that far. The snow is pretty stable. Just a little slipping."

"Are we taking the snowmobile we have here or hitching a ride?"

Lloyd said, "We'll be going back with them, getting this snowmobile up to the top of the snow will take some doing and I'm ready to go, aren't you?"

"Oh yeah. Can we leave now?"

Thomas said, "Yes. Tracy, you ride with Pete, he's the head man."

She didn't really want to ride with some stranger, but she wanted to get off the damn mountain, and would have taken a ride from a polar bear. Lloyd seemed just as eager as he climbed on the back with the other guy, bringing the rifle with him.

It only took a few minutes to get up to the road. They waved goodbye to the rescuers and Tracy and Brenda climbed into the backseat while the guys loaded the snowmobile into the bed of the truck.

Brenda whispered, "Did you and Lloyd…"

"You don't have to whisper; they can't hear us. But no, we were too worried about the guy who started the avalanche to get undressed again."

"That sucks, but I guess I would be concerned too. Don't want to get caught with your pants down, as they say."

"Exactly. We rigged up a noisemaker that would have woken the dead, but we didn't want to take any chances."

Brenda nodded. "I noticed when we got close enough to see, that Lloyd had the rifle and you had a death grip on your rock hammer."

"Yeah, we didn't know for sure if the people coming were friendly or not."

Brenda hugged her tight, again. "I was so worried about you."

"We were fine, there was plenty of sleeping bags and blankets, and food and lights, even power banks to charge a half dozen phones. It really is well-equipped. Not that I wanted to stay any longer than necessary, you understand."

"Totally."

The men opened the doors and slid in, and they were off down the road. Tracy breathed a sigh of relief. She couldn't wait for a nice hot shower and some clean clothes.

Taking the forest road took a lot longer than cross-country did, but Tracy was content to wait while they wound around and over to the highway that ran through Granby. After that it was only about a half hour to the ranch.

When they pulled in, several ranch hands and some of the family were gathered in the yard to welcome them back.

Alyssa went with Tracy to her room to check her knee. Brenda wasn't ready to leave her friend's side and followed them. Alyssa agreed it was probably only hyper-extended but advised to be gentle with it. "Once a joint has been hyper-extended it's more vulnerable to that type of injury. More concerning, however, is being trapped under all that snow. How is your mental state?"

Tears welled in her eyes, but she didn't let them fall. Tracy tried to laugh it off, "I wouldn't recommend it."

Brenda took one hand and Alyssa the other and they just waited.

"I was so scared. I was so afraid I'd be swept down the mountain, then I got ahold of the tree, but all that snow kept coming and coming, covering me."

Her breath shuddered and she zeroed in on Brenda. "In an instant, my mind went back to that avalanche show we watched. And I was scared about running out of oxygen, I tried to make an air pocket between me and the tree."

One tear escaped and trailed down her cheek. "I don't know how long it would have lasted, but Lloyd found me fast enough. I used my rock hammer on my specimen container to make a noise he could follow so that I didn't have to shout and use more air."

A second tear escaped. "I know it wasn't a long time before he had me freed, but it seemed like forever. I just kept on believing he would save me, and he did."

Brenda and Alyssa, both hugged her. She felt more loved in that moment, than she had in her whole life.

CHAPTER 14

*T*he whole family and all the engineers came together for dinner and to hear about Tracy and Lloyd's experience on the mountain. There was a lot of speculation about the avalanche, even though the Forest Service said it wasn't natural.

Tracy had to agree that it seemed pretty farfetched and a ridiculous way to keep people away. If the reclamation crew couldn't get to the mine, why would anyone else be able to? Even the highly skilled mountain experts had balked at the idea of going in that first day.

"If it was someone that caused it, they don't know shit about our mountains," Grandpa K stated.

No one disagreed with that.

Travis nodded, "True, dad. I think we should put up some surveillance cameras just to keep an eye on things. We've got those hunting cameras we bought and never used, thanks to Rachel, and her camera, spotting the drone."

Rachel beamed at Travis. Adam and Beau grinned at each other and Beau said, "What a fun day that was, discovering the drone guy had been following the map we'd made for the twins' birthday."

Cade and Chase high fived each other across the table. "Best birthday ever."

Katie shifted in her chair, probably trying to alleviate some of the baby pressure, she was as big as a house and not due for a few more weeks. "We'll be coming up with party ideas for our own kids now."

Chase put a hand on her back and Katie leaned into it with a sigh.

Summer rubbed her baby belly, "Not for a couple of years."

"More time to plan," Cade winked at his brother, and laid a hand on his wife's baby mound, moving his hand in soothing circles.

Travis cleared his throat, "Back to the topic. We've got those cameras we can set up around the site and inside the mine, to see if anyone outside of those present, is moving around up there."

Lloyd nodded. "As soon as its stable enough up there to be walking around in the trees, we can put them up. There are a couple of locations that would give us a good view of the mine entrance."

Thomas agreed, "Yep, you and I can do that, Lloyd. If the whole damn place wasn't covered in snow, we might have been able to scout around to see if someone has been watching us. The avalanche nixes that idea."

"Although if someone has been there since the avalanche it would be pretty obvious," Lloyd pointed out.

Thomas nodded. "True, but if they have been out there with the snow as unstable as it is they are idiots and will probably take themselves out of the picture. Natural selection and all that."

Cade said, "If it was bear season, for sure, but since they are hibernating now..."

"Cats would do the job," Chase speculated.

Travis cleared his throat. "Back to the topic. Again." Then he looked at Meg. "Who invited those two?"

Meg smiled. "You did, honey."

"Darn it. What was I thinking?" He frowned at his sons, who grinned back at him, he shook his head and his lips twitched in amusement. Turning back to the table at large, Travis said, "If Thomas and Lloyd take the cameras up in a few days maybe we can get a handle on things."

Matt said, with a grin that looked suspicious to Tracy, "That sounds like a fine plan. I wanted to mention how helpful Lloyd has been to our team."

Conor shook his head. "Now is not the time."

"I think it is the perfect time."

"Matt, no."

Tracy's stomach dropped as Matt ignored Conner and resumed talking. "Lloyd has taught himself all about our methods and the geology of this area."

Beau said, "That doesn't surprise me in the least. He's educated himself on every area of running a ranch, including some of the veterinary techniques we use."

Lloyd was glad to hear Beau's assessment and dearly hoped he was wrong about where Matt was going with this discussion. He didn't want the whole family to hear about Matt's hairbrained idea.

Matt nodded at Beau, then turned his attention to Travis. "Our company would like to sponsor him to get certified in mine reclamation. There is a program near the college, just two short hours away from here. I took the liberty of talking to the head of the program about Lloyd's learning disability and he said that they would be able to accommodate him with verbal exams."

Matt kept talking but his voice became a buzz in Lloyd's ears. He could not believe the audacity of the guy. He'd told Matt no, clearly and concisely. He gritted his teeth and tried to get his mouth to work through the fury. "Matt, I told you I wasn't interested. I have a job."

Tracy jumped in, "I heard him tell you no."

Cade said, "That's an awesome opportunity, you really should think about it."

Other murmurs were shared around the table until the noise became a blur in his mind and little Emily banged on her highchair to join in.

Grandpa K tapped his knife on his plate, and everyone stilled. "I don't think this is a discussion for the whole family. It's up to Lloyd." He looked pointedly at every person around the table one by one. Finally, turning his attention to Lloyd. "But if you are interested, son, don't let the ranch hold you back. You do good work here, but we would never want to keep you from your full potential."

Travis nodded. "We've discussed the idea, Lloyd and we would miss you but if you need to fly higher than this ranch, we'll be behind you."

Lloyd frowned. They had discussed it? "How did you know about it? I haven't mentioned it to anyone." He turned his glare on the engineers.

Matt held up his hands. "I didn't say anything until tonight."

Tracy cleared her throat and her expression told him the story before she said a thing. "I, um, mentioned it to Grandpa

93

K. I thought… I shouldn't have… I'm sorry. I… I'm just sorry."

Tears filled her eyes, but he hardened his heart against them, and stood. "If you'll all excuse me, I need some air."

Tracy gasped, but he ignored her and walked out of the room. He pulled on his boots and coat and went out into the night. He'd been ambushed by Matt, but even worse than that was the fact that Tracy had betrayed him.

Why had she talked to Grandpa K about Matt running his mouth? Travis and at least Grandpa K had talked about the possibility of him leaving. He had no plans to leave, he thought Matt's idea was ridiculous.

That wasn't quite the truth, because he *had* looked up the certification online, but that didn't mean he was planning to do anything about it. Now Matt had forced his hand, and everyone seemed to think it was a great idea. Well, the hell with that, it wasn't their ass on the line.

The problem was, Lloyd was afraid to fail. He'd barely made it through high school. How could he possibly try something like this? If he failed, would he have to pay the engineering company back? Probably, they weren't going to pay for someone that they couldn't put to work to make it worth the investment.

He muttered and swore about the whole thing as he marched along the road toward town. His mind whirled with anger one minute and possibilities the next. He didn't know how long he walked, but when he started to see the lights from town, he decided he had better turn around. Either that or keep right on going until he hit the bar. He could get roaring drunk.

CHAPTER 15

*T*racy had screwed up big time. She'd wanted to go after Lloyd, but Meg had put a hand on her arm to keep her from going. "Come help me in the kitchen, Tracy." Then to the room Meg said, "We'll be right back with dessert."

When they got to the kitchen, Meg said softly, "He needs time."

"But I shouldn't have said anything. He's mad at me."

"He was put on the spot in front of the whole family. It's the whole situation he's mad about, not just you."

"I know but I betrayed him."

"Maliciously?"

"No of course not, Brenda and I were having dinner with Grandpa K and it just came out."

"Then give him some time to think it through. When he's ready he'll come to you."

Hope filled Tracy. "Do you think so?"

"He's lived here all his adult life and half of his child-hood. I know him pretty well."

"I hope you're right." She felt her cheeks heat, but continued, "I was hoping he would join me in my room tonight. Now I've screwed that up."

"So, you and Lloyd have gotten cozy, have you?"

"Yeah, he was going to mention it to Travis, I think."

"No need, you're both adults. We don't have a gatekeeper on the doors."

"Thanks. Do you really think he'll forgive me for running my mouth?"

"I do. He's a magnanimous person. Now help me get the cake cut up and on plates."

As she helped Meg in the kitchen, she hoped that Lloyd would pardon her. She'd been stupid to tell Grandpa K and maybe even Brenda. Although Matt blurting it out tonight had caused a ruckus. The fact that Grandpa K and Travis had known about it and hadn't been blindsided, she saw as a good thing. Maybe Lloyd would get to that conclusion eventually.

By the time Lloyd had walked back to the ranch he was calm, cold, and wished he'd stayed for dessert. He'd seen the cake earlier and had started thinking about it. He knew he could go in and take a slice, but he wasn't sure he wanted to run into anyone. His sweet tooth outweighed his hesitancy to see people. It was late evening and he hoped everyone was settled in their own pursuits, thankfully the engineering team had gone back to the cabin and their trailers.

The kids and their families would be back in their own homes. So, the number of people in the house would be small. He went in through the mudroom, leaving his boots and jacket behind. His feet were sore from all the walking so when he finally took off his boots it felt good.

The kitchen was nearly empty, Grandpa K sat at the

kitchen table with a cup of coffee and a book. Lloyd was fairly certain the man was waiting for him. How Grandpa K knew he would come in was a mystery.

Lloyd nodded at the man. "Grandpa K."

"Lloyd. Get yourself a piece of that cake, it is delicious. Coffee is hot and decaf."

Apparently, Grandpa K had something on his mind. Lloyd did as he was told. "Do you want another slice of cake?"

"Naw, one is enough for today. Might have some with my breakfast in the morning." His eyes twinkled with mischief.

"Sounds like a plan." Lloyd sat across from the old guy. He knew whatever Grandpa K had to say would be good council.

"Matt blindsided you tonight, he's still young and impetuous."

Lloyd figured the guy was a couple of years older than himself, but he didn't interrupt to say so.

"His idea is something you should consider carefully. It's an opportunity that doesn't come around every day. I'm not saying you should or shouldn't do it, just that you need to think about it seriously. You'll always have a place here on the Rockin' K, but you've got a fine mind and if you feel a leaning toward learning about the mine reclamation field, you might want to look into it."

Lloyd *did* like the work they were doing, he liked helping to clean up a hazardous environment. But he didn't know how he would do at the school. He stuffed his face with cake, so he didn't have to respond right away. He didn't like showing his insecurities.

It was as if Grandpa K could hear his thoughts. "I think you'd do just fine in the program. Going into it knowing your limitations and how to compensate for them would be completely different from public education, son. Plus, it's only a one-year program, you can tough anything out for a year."

Lloyd put his fork down. "I can admit it sounds interesting. But the fear of failing is high."

"Sometimes fear is the very thing that points us in the direction we should go. It indicates that our mind is ready to move."

Lloyd took another bite of cake and washed it down with coffee. He didn't know what else to say, he had some thinking to do.

"You'd be able to see Tracy."

Lloyd frowned; he wasn't happy with Tracy at the moment.

"Don't be hard on the girl. I asked her how her day had gone, and she told me about what Matt had said and how angry she'd been at him putting you on the spot. She cares for you a great deal and that's kind of a foreign feeling for her. She doesn't quite know how to handle it."

Lloyd sighed, Grandpa K was right, she didn't have a lot of practice with love and affection. "I just don't like being talked about."

"I'm the one that decided to talk it over with Travis. I wanted us to be on the same page if you decided to pursue it or if Matt brought it up again, which he did. I know that him butting in is frustrating, but he really believes you would be a great asset to the company. That's not a bad thing, you should take it as a compliment."

Lloyd didn't think some guy pushing him into something was very complimentary.

"Just don't be hard on the girl. She wanted to come after you, but Meg derailed that. Tracy is probably sitting up in her room worried you're going to stay angry, or desert her, she's not had many people stick by her."

He knew that was the case and he wasn't going to be someone like her foster families had been. "I'm not mad at her. She didn't do anything malicious."

"No, she didn't. Maybe you should go up and let her know that."

"Maybe I will."

TRACY WAS TRYING HER BEST TO WORK ON HER CLASS assignments, but her mind wouldn't settle on the task. Worry about Lloyd being angry with her kept pushing its way into her thoughts. Fortunately, her homework didn't require a steady stream of consciousness, they were individual problems. So, she was alternating between solving the equations and fretting about Lloyd. Not an optimal way to study but at least she was making some progress.

The knock on the door had her abandoning her work to rush to the door.

"Lloyd, are you still mad at me? I'm so sorry I ran my mouth. I was just so angry with Matt for putting you on the spot and Grandpa K—"

He wiped the tears from her face that she didn't realize were there.

Pulling her into his arms and backing her into her room, he kicked the door closed behind him. "Shh, baby. It's okay, I know you weren't trying to hurt me. Grandpa K explained what happened."

Relief filled her and her body sagged against him, she'd been so tense. So scared to lose one of her closest friends. They moved to the bed where he sat next to her with his arm around her shoulders. She said, "I kind of hate Matt right now."

"I was feeling the same, angry and blind-sided, until I got almost to town, then I realized it was a compliment. Delivered badly, but he really sees potential in me. Maybe I need to seriously consider it."

"It would be a big step, leaving the ranch, trying something completely new and different." She didn't want to discourage him. "I think you would breeze right through the program. If you want to be an engineer, it would be a great entry point."

"I'm not making any decisions tonight. I wanted to come make sure you knew I wasn't angry at you."

"Are you 'not angry' enough to spend the night?"

"I don't have any clean clothes for the morning."

She walked her fingers up his chest. "Those are clean enough, at least to get back to the bunkhouse. There are no plans to go up to the mine tomorrow. They want to give it another day or two. Travis mentioned getting the cameras out with you and Thomas after lunch. So, we wouldn't have to hurry."

He grabbed her hand before she started unbuttoning his shirt. "You drive a hard bargain."

He pulled her into his arms and kissed her slowly, her whole body relaxed from the fear that had held her captive since dinner, but it didn't take long before it lit back up with desire.

Little by little clothes hit the floor, her shirt and bra first. Then she managed to get his shirt off of him. The first flesh on flesh contact was marvelous. Her curves fit into the planes of his body like they'd been sculpted together then carefully separated.

She reveled in the slight friction from the hair on his chest on her sensitive nipples. She rubbed them back and forth until he groaned and pulled her in tighter where she couldn't move, his lips slamming down on hers.

She melted into him, her muscles going loose and soft. His arms around her held her up as he backed her toward the bed. When her legs bumped into the mattress, he unfastened her jeans and slid them and her panties down in one swift move.

He urged her back to sit on the bed while he quickly divested himself of his jeans and boxers, leaving his erection hard and yearning toward her. She gladly took hold of it, running her hand up and down its length, the skin so soft over the steel beneath it.

Before she could do more, he pulled her fully onto the bed with him beside her. He took both her hands and raised them above her head.

"If you don't stop that, this is going to be over too soon."

"We've got all night, and as I recall you recover pretty fast, cowboy."

He laughed and groaned at the same time. "That may be true, but being inside you is always better."

She spread her legs. "Welcome."

"Are you sure you don't want to use protection? I've got some in the bunkhouse."

"Too late for that. I'm not letting you get away."

He didn't join with her right away. He started kissing her again, his hand moving down between her legs, stroking the little bundle of nerves he found there. Pleasure swamped her, lighting little fires along her skin. Moisture flooded her sex, readying her for him.

When he finally did enter her, it was glorious. They moved together in the age-old dance of mating. Slowly they climbed toward the stars, until frenzy overtook them, and their bodies demanded release. Movements became almost frantic as he pounded into her, and she answered back, arching up to meet him stroke for stroke.

The release shattered them both, her body milked him dry as their consciousness became shards of light that vied for brilliance with the stars. They drifted as light together in the atmosphere.

Slowly they began to coalesce back into wholeness, him keeping a few pieces of her light as she kept a few of his, forever to be bound. She found that thought comforting and smiled sleepily. Lloyd pulled the blankets up over their cooling bodies as slumber overtook them.

CHAPTER 16

The whole team finally made it back up to the mine a week later. Thomas and Lloyd had gone up the day before to place the cameras and bring down the snowmobile they'd left behind. They didn't think anything looked disturbed.

Tracy had used the time at the ranch to work on school homework, and had tested the samples she'd been taking when the avalanche hit.

Lloyd was busy during the day with ranch work and looking at his own samples, but he joined her every evening after dinner, and they spent the night wrapped up in each other. Tracy loved every minute.

She'd never shared a bed with a man before and that took some getting used to. Lloyd was a big guy and took up a lot of room. But she managed to curl herself up next to him and sleep just fine. Of course, the reason might be because she was exhausted after all their amorous activities.

Tracy could admit that the return to the mine spiked her anxiety. She wasn't about to let her fear show, but her hands were cold inside her gloves and her heart raced.

After they arrived at the mine Lloyd took her hand. "Don't be worried, we'll be just fine."

"How could you tell?"

"You're trembling and your face is pale. I don't think the idiot that started the avalanche will be doing anything like that any time soon. He lost as much time here as we did."

Tracy looked around. "But don't you think he'll try something else?"

"I do, but I doubt it will be confrontational, he's been hiding. I don't think he's just going to waltz out here and make himself known. Especially since he's breaking the law."

"He seems pretty desperate, what if he gets crazy?"

"Like shoot everyone? I don't think that's going to happen. I don't think he wants to go to jail. I can't quite figure out what he's up to. We noticed earlier that there were some new scrapings at the back of the cave, but not enough to look like he's working the mine."

Tracy agreed, "Yeah, I wondered about that too. I did see some places where it looked like holes had been dug, but then filled back in."

"Do you think he's on a treasure hunt?"

"It would make the most sense. Obviously, we're not going to leave the mine in its current condition, but if he could get a few days where we weren't here, he might be able to find what he's looking for."

"That's a very interesting idea, show me the holes you're talking about. I wasn't looking at the floor of the cave, just the walls."

She laughed. "Well, I'm closer to the ground than you are."

He tapped her nose. "That you are."

The engineers had started clearing away the debris from the avalanche so they could get back to working with the microbes. Lloyd said, "We'll join you in a minute, Tracy has an idea I want to investigate. If we find something interesting, we'll come get you." He followed Tracy into the mine.

SHE WENT OVER AND SQUATTED DOWN. "THIS IS THE FIRST one I noticed, because the ground is still kind of soft, but there are more, and they seem to be in a straight line." She pointed to the ones that she was referring to. They looked carefully over the rest of the cave floor.

"I think it's more than a straight line," he said. "I think it's a grid, there obviously aren't any holes where it's bedrock, but there's plenty of other ones every few feet. Let's check the first one. We can dig down and see how deep it is."

It was about two feet deep and a foot and a half square. Lloyd said, "Let's leave it open to show the rest of them."

Tracy nodded. "Let's mark the rest of the holes, so they can see the full effect."

They went around the floor of the cave, marking the spots that looked like they'd been dug. There were quite a few of them, even some in the extra little room that someone had been sleeping in. "I think you may be on to something, Tracy. That's a lot of digging and very little mining. I wonder if the outside of the cave has the same pattern?"

Tracy said, "Like they started in the mine and then expanded when they didn't find what they were looking for?"

Lloyd nodded. "Exactly. I think we should show the others. I'll go get them."

Tracy hoped they wouldn't think she was an idiot. When she'd first discovered it, she wondered if she should tell them. But whatever someone was looking for wasn't as important as getting the tailings cleaned up, so she hadn't mentioned it.

Now that the guy had escalated, it might be important information to have.

When they were all in the cave and around the first hole, Lloyd said, "Tracy noticed this network of holes in the ground. We were thinking that maybe what the perpetrator is up to is looking for something that was buried. Not working on the mine."

Matt said, "That makes better sense. I couldn't figure out why there wasn't more new-looking mining activity."

"Yeah, and if they were doing actual mining then why would they have disturbed the tailings? Great observation, Tracy." Connor said.

Tracy flushed with pride. "We've marked all the holes that we could find. And you can see it's a very distinctive grid except for wherever it's bedrock. Same in the extra little room off to the side."

Julian, the younger geologist said, "Well, that's not exactly why we're here. We're here to clean up the tailings not to determine what the guy is up to."

"True, but if the reason the guy disturbed the tailing is to find buried treasure, then that tells us a lot about his expertise and intentions," Thomas said.

"So, we should look outside the mine and see if we can find the same kind of pattern. If we do find a pattern, we might want to move the cameras based on where it looks like he's already dug," Connor said.

"That's a good plan," Thomas said.

Lloyd and Tracy filled up their hole and went out with the others, once the debris from the avalanche was cleaned up, they could continue work on the tailings and also look for more places that had been dug into. They didn't want the avalanche to set them back too far on their time schedule.

LLOYD WAS SO PROUD OF TRACY TO HAVE FOUND THAT BIT OF evidence, it gave them a whole different perspective on what might be happening here. It would certainly indicate why the tailings had gotten disrupted, if the guy was trying to dig near the area, he might not even know what he was getting into.

Based on the newly-mined area inside, it didn't look like he had any expertise. He'd just chopped away at the far back wall which meant he might not even know what to look for. If something had been buried, that was a completely different scenario. If somebody buried a treasure near or under the mine tailings that would just be stupid. It had poisonous minerals and the miners would have known that, but Lloyd didn't know if the new guy did. He had to wonder if there was a bunch of gold buried somewhere.

As he thought through some of the assumptions they were going by, if all of a sudden someone had been called back to the war, it wouldn't have been wise to carry a bunch of gold with him. Burying it and then coming back to retrieve it later would have been a much smarter idea.

Lloyd figured someone had heard stories, but they hadn't been specific, at least not specific enough to find the buried treasure. Stories that were passed down from generations also lost a lot of detail, while at the same time expounded on areas that weren't the correct information. So it could be that a handful of gold had turned into a huge box of gold. It was hard to say.

CHAPTER 17

a few days later, Tracy startled and quickly looked up and over at Lloyd, "Did you hear that?"

"Yeah, I did."

"Was that a wild cat?"

"A mountain lion? Sure sounded like one."

"What do we do?"

"Probably nothing. They don't usually attack large groups of people. You all might want to go into the mine for a bit. Thomas and I will go check it out."

"You will?"

"Yes." He grabbed the rifle and went over to where Thomas was working with Brenda. Thomas was staring off in the direction the sound had come from.

"You heard the cat?"

"Yeah, funny time of year for it though."

"That's what I was thinking, and time of day, too. And no answer from a male."

"We should still go check," Thomas said.

"Agreed. I got the rifle."

Thomas said, "Brenda, you and the engineers might want

to stick together, no cougar is going to attack six people. You could go in the mine for more safety if you want. Lloyd, let's go."

Thomas and Lloyd started toward the direction they'd heard the sound come from.

Thomas said, "I'll look for tracks and scat on the ground. You keep your eyes on the trees and look for scratches."

Lloyd checked the trees as they walked. If a cat was marking its territory, the trees would be scratched. Mountain lions could mate any time of year so it was plausible that a female could be in the area looking for a male, but they'd heard no answering call.

They weren't noisy animals. Only when they were mating. They kept moving through the forest and they didn't hear the call again. Lloyd and Thomas saw no scratches on the ground or any scat. There was no half-eaten, half-buried food. All the signs of a wild cat in the area were missing.

Lloyd pointed out a tree. "There's scratches on that one."

They went in close and looked carefully. Thomas said, "Yeah there are scratches but…"

Lloyd said, "But what?"

"Well, they just don't look quite right."

"Oh yeah?" Lloyd asked.

"No. I mean a cat can get rambunctious like that and make lots of scratches. But not always. Sometimes they just make a few claw marks just to mark their territory. And there should be other evidence like footprints, or scat, or a catch with scratches on the ground. I didn't see any, and I was watching," Thomas said.

Thomas paced back and forth in front of the tree, speaking almost to himself as he worked it out. "That was a mating call. But I didn't hear the answer from the male, and why else would a female cry out like that, when there's no male in the vicinity?"

Thomas looked him in the eye, so Lloyd shrugged. "I don't know."

"Something looks a little fishy to me."

"Maybe we should keep going to see if there's anything else to be found."

"Yeah, that would be good, for a few minutes, but I don't want to leave everyone back at the mine worried."

"Good point," Lloyd said.

They kept walking, circling around where they had found the tree scratchings, they didn't find anything else.

Lloyd said, "Maybe we should put a camera out here. We don't have any out this far."

"That's not a bad idea."

"We could get the one out of the mine. Since Tracy found the grid of holes, I don't think they need to go in there unless he wants to camp out and use the cave as shelter."

Thomas nodded, "I agree."

"We could always get another camera, if we feel like we need to put one back in the mine."

"Let's get back, get the camera and put it out here."

It didn't take them long to get back to the mine, where they told the engineers what they found.

Thomas said, "It looks like cats, but not quite. Cats only make those sounds during mating season. So, there should have been a male and a female call. The female starts it and then the male should have answered, which didn't happen. We found scratches on a tree, but they didn't quite look right. And there were no footprints, or scratches on the ground, or any scat, or anything else that might indicate a mountain lion was in the vicinity."

Lloyd continued. "We're going to take the camera that's in the mine out, so that it has a view of that area."

"So, you don't think it's a cat?" Tracy asked.

Thomas ran his hand around the back of his neck. "I can't say for sure. But I don't think so. It doesn't look or feel quite right."

"Do you think it's the guy trying to scare us off?" Connor asked.

Thomas nodded. "Could be, it's a much smarter way to handle it. Trying to scare us off with animal noises, rather than sending a couple tons of snow down on top of us."

Lloyd lifted the rifle. "But we'll keep the weapon handy, just in case."

Thomas put his hands on his hips. "Mountain lions are not real big on coming up and being around a bunch of people. One small defenseless or injured person maybe, if game was scarce, but not eight people. And game isn't scarce, the newly born cattle would be a better target than a human, but even that isn't likely. There are plenty of deer, raccoons, and smaller animals up here."

"Well, that's good to know," Brenda said.

Tracy couldn't agree more. Knowing that did not help her feeling of anxiety, however. She was jumpy and nervous the rest of the day, looking around, listening intently, nearly jumping out of her skin at every small sound. She was a wreck by the time they called it a day. The trip down the mountain on the snowmobiles was the only thing that finally allowed her to relax.

When Thomas and Lloyd said they needed to report the incident to Travis, Tracy was thrilled, she wanted a few minutes alone with Brenda. She grabbed her friend's hand before she could get sidetracked with dinner or anything else and hauled her up to their rooms. She yanked Brenda into her room and shut the door with a bang.

"Tracy, what's the rush?"

"I don't know how long the guys will be in with Travis and I need to talk to you, alone."

Brenda sat on Tracy's bed and started pulling off the outer wear she had on. "All right talk."

"I'm scared. I don't want to go back up there tomorrow."

"Tomorrow is Thursday and your class day; you never go up on Thursday."

Tracy didn't want to hear logic; she was freaking out here. "Fine, I don't want to go up on Friday then."

"But the guys said—"

She cut her friend off. "I know what they said, but what if they're wrong? What if one of us goes off for a potty break and gets mauled by some wild animal."

"Trace, it's probably just the guy trying to scare us."

"Mission accomplished."

"Do you really want to be scared off by a tape recording and some guy with a knife carving up a tree?" Brenda asked.

"No, but what if it's not some guy, but a real animal."

"In that case the animal is a lot more scared of you, than you are of it."

"I'm not sure that's true. I'm pretty scared," Tracy demanded.

"Tracy."

"No, I mean it. I'm a city girl, muggers I can handle, I've taken self-defense classes. Crazy drivers, no prob. Wild animals I have no idea. I think I'm in the wrong career."

"Don't be silly. You're almost ready to graduate, don't chicken out now. Besides, the Forest Service or somebody probably has some kind of wildlife classes to teach people how to handle encounters. We should look into it. I could probably benefit from something like that myself."

Tracy rushed over to her laptop. "Let's check online."

"How about we get ready and have dinner first. You can check later tonight or tomorrow on your class day. You might find something interesting for your thesis even."

Tracy didn't want to wait, but then her stomach growled, and Lloyd knocked on her door. "Dinner in ten minutes. Meet you down there."

She called out, "Okay," then turned to her friend, "All right, I'll check tomorrow."

"Good, because I am starving." Brenda squeezed Tracy's hand. "Don't worry, we won't let anything use you as a snack."

At dinner Travis brought up the subject of the possible cougar. "I think you should all wait until Monday to return to the mine. Give the cameras time to capture footage. Thomas doesn't believe it looks authentic, but I think we should make sure."

"Why?" Connor asked.

Travis continued, "The observed behavior was not consistent. Which means one of two things, either the information gathered was planted, or we have a rogue animal. I want to know which it is before you risk yourselves. I've called the National Forest Rangers and have alerted them. Thomas and Lloyd will meet them on the upper road in the morning and take them down to show them what was discovered."

Thomas nodded. "We should give them a few days to investigate. I know what to look for, but I am not an expert and as Travis pointed out we don't know what might happen if it is a rogue animal."

Discussion continued around the table, but Tracy wasn't

listening, she felt great relief at the idea of professionals looking into the possibility of mountain lions before they returned to the mine. Travis had been wise to caution them on staying away for a few days on the off chance it was dangerous.

She was still going to look up and see what she could find about what to do if encountering a mountain lion, and any other predatory wildlife for that matter. If she was going to choose a career where there could be wild animal exposure, she needed to know what to do and how to handle it.

The knowledge could save her life, but more importantly it would keep her from acting like a scared little girl. She wondered if she should invest in some kind of weapon and take lessons on its use.

Lloyd might be a good one to talk to about that, he wasn't the least bit hesitant around the rifle. She didn't know that she wanted to carry around a rifle to every job, but if they had one on a work site, like they did here, it would be a good thing to know how to use. At the very least some safety lessons would be in order, rather than just staying away from it.

Tracy decided to ask Lloyd about it and then convince Brenda to join her in any education that could be had here at the ranch. A couple of city girls with no wildlife preparation were just begging for trouble. In her mind it would be a valuable class for the school to offer. Even if it was billed as an after-school club.

CHAPTER 18

*R*ay slammed into the log cabin he was sharing with his brother at the Singing River Ranch. His brother was lounging on the bed in his skivvies. "Have you lost your frigging mind? A cougar? Seriously? You don't know a damned thing about a mountain lion. You'd have been better off trying to convince them there was an alligator roaming around. At least you know *something* about those."

Buddy grinned, "Obviously it worked if you know about it. Did they turn tail and run? Can we go in tomorrow and start looking?"

"No dumbass, all your stunts are accomplishing is causing them to put more cameras out. They've now moved one from inside the mine to the area where you scratched up the tree. They called us to let us know that they believe someone is pretending to be a mountain lion."

"Fuck."

"The Forest Rangers will be combing the area looking for a rogue cougar all weekend. Because, idiot brother of mine, you didn't leave enough evidence, so on the off chance there is an animal they need to know because it is acting irrationally."

"What do you mean?"

"You used a female mating call. The sound they only use in heat and when a male is nearby. There was no answer from a male."

Buddy shrugged. "No big deal, so she was confused."

Ray paced, ticking points off his fingers. "You also left no footprints. No scratches on the ground or any hidden food. And the biggest one of all no scat."

"What is scat?"

"Shit, moron. A female in heat also sprays her scent."

"I don't have no cougar shit. Or no female spray."

"Which is why you should have never started this mess. If you hadn't tried to run them off, we could have gone in over the weekend when they weren't working on the tailings and looked in places where the cameras were not pointed. Now the place will be covered in rangers, and I have to work all weekend, thank-you very much."

"You never said we could go in on the weekend."

"I was making sure it would be free and clear first. Which now it is not. I hope you didn't leave any evidence behind."

"Nope, nothing to worry about on that front."

Ray watched his brother carefully, he was lying about something, but Ray couldn't tell what it was. "I'm going to change out of my uniform and go get us something to eat."

"Let's go out together," Buddy stood and rubbed his belly.

Ray stripped off his ranger shirt and sniffed at the armpits, it could go one more day before washing it, so he hung it up in the closet. "No can do, no one knows we're together and we need to keep it that way."

"Dammit, I can't stand being in this dump alone all the time."

"You could get a job." He stepped out of the uniform pants and grabbed some jeans, thank God, Buddy and he did not wear the same size. Buddy had a pile of clothes the size of Mount Everest in the corner, and the place stunk of sweat.

Buddy laughed. "No fucking way. I would stand out like a sore thumb. Besides I don't know what kind of job I could get."

"Anything. Trash hauler. Dish washer. Road sign holder, I heard that road repairs start soon, the frigid weather up at this elevation causes a lot of road damage so there's always road work. Holding one of those signs probably pays pretty good."

"Because it's boring as hell. And fucking colder than shit. No way." Buddy flopped back onto his bed. "Just go get us some food, asshole."

"You need to do laundry, brother, and air this place out, it stinks. For that matter, while I'm gone getting food, take a shower, that might help."

"Fuck you."

"I mean it, shower or I'll eat both your meal and mine."

BUDDY SWORE AND THREW HIS WATER BOTTLE AT THE DOOR. His brother was a bossy motherfucker, but he never issued idle threats. That meant he had to shower. He sniffed his armpit. He did stink, not that he gave a shit. There was no one around to impress.

He stomped to the bathroom; he didn't have any clean skivvies, so he'd have to wear the same ones he had on. He'd run out of clean clothes a few days ago, he supposed he'd have to do laundry. Maybe he'd take a run into Granby to get out of this nosy little town, or even go a little further, to Fraser, he could use some new scenery. Hot Sulphur Springs or Kremmling would be a good drive. Yeah, he'd load up his laundry and take a drive tomorrow, while his asshole brother was at work.

Him get a job? Holding some damn sign on the side of the road? No fucking way. He just needed a better plan to get those assholes away from the mine so they could keep looking for the treasure.

He needed his brother to foot the bill on this excursion. Once he found the gold his interfering brother might meet with some horrible accident.

Buddy had no intention of sharing.

R AY TRIED TO CALM DOWN AS HE DROVE INTO TOWN TO THE café. They had good food and it was reasonably priced. The waitress was an older lady with kids who he liked chatting with, if she wasn't too busy.

He pulled up in front of the restaurant and went in to find a completely different woman working the place. The waitress with name tag reading Jen smiled at him and all the thoughts in his head escaped, she was so pretty, and the smile was killer. "Just one tonight?"

He glanced around the restaurant while he tried to get his brain to engage, it was nearly empty. "Um yeah, but when I finish, I'll take an order to go." Before she got the wrong impression he quickly said, "My brother wanted to shower so I'm taking food back for him."

"Follow me."

He'd follow her anywhere she wanted to go. Her long blonde hair was pulled up in a high, curly ponytail that bounced as they walked. He figured she was about five foot four or five, a good six inches from his five-eleven frame. She obviously had some Asian descent; he was going to guess Chinese. The blonde hair indicated to him she either dyed it or she wasn't full Asian.

Jen pointed him to his seat, and he took it. She laid a menu on the table in front of him. "You've got a bit of a southern accent. There's a customer that's been coming in on my normal shift during the day that has a similar one, but his is much more pronounced. Any relation to Buddy Bodine?"

"That all depends on if he's been pleasant or a pain in the, um, neck."

"He's been okay, asks me out every time he comes in. That gets a little annoying because he's not my type."

She hadn't said she was unavailable, and he knew how to treat a lady, unlike his brother. "If you won't hold it against me, yes, he's my younger brother, I'm Ray Bodine. Nice to meet you. Maybe I'll have to switch to the night shift so I can come in while you're working. I work for the Forest Service during the day."

She smiled her pretty smile again and Ray's mouth went dry. He forced a swallow and then thought to ask, "Where is Mary tonight? I hope everything is okay."

"Everything is fine, we switched shifts, it's her son's birthday, they are having a family party tonight, and then a sleepover with eight kids on Saturday. I'll be working a lot this weekend as Mary rides herd on the boys."

"Good to know. Unfortunately, we're all working over-time this weekend, or I would be eating every meal here."

Her eyes sparkled but she said, "It's not good to eat every meal out, and it gets expensive. Now what can I get you to drink?"

"How about some tea, if you could just dip your finger in it, I know it will be sweet as can be."

Her cheeks took on a rosy hue. "That would be a health code violation, but we do have some sweet tea already made up."

He sighed dramatically. "I suppose that will have to do."

She laughed. "You Bodine boys are quite the charmers."

"I hope you like me better than Buddy."

Turning to go she said, "We'll see, now look over that menu and I'll be back with your tea."

As she sashayed off, Ray decided he'd be in after his weekend shift. If she was working doubles, he'd still be able to see her.

CHAPTER 19

*L*loyd noticed Tracy was quiet during dinner. Something was on her mind. He hoped she wasn't too worried about the mountain lion; they were very reticent animals. He'd only seen a single glimpse of one in his whole life. Unlike other creatures they stayed far away from mankind.

Tracy could probably use some wildlife education, even if just the two of them talked about it when they were together. In his opinion turning a bunch of city kids out into the world to work in the mineral science industries which often included the wilderness seemed pretty foolish.

He figured some of them probably came from ranches or other outdoor lifestyles, but a lot came from cities, too. Hell, even a rattlesnake was deadly for someone who didn't know what to do if they encountered one.

He touched her knee to gain her attention. "Can we talk after dinner?"

"Yes, there are some things I want to discuss," she gifted him with a beautiful smile, and he knew it wouldn't be easy to talk, rather than moving on to more interesting pursuits.

Maybe they should talk in a public area before moving to her room.

He wondered if she was thinking the same thing when she said, "Can we have Brenda and Thomas if he wants to join us? I want to talk something over with you and them."

"Certainly."

Brenda was sitting on the other side of Tracy, and they had a low conversation before Tracy turned back. "We'll all meet in my room after dinner cleanup."

Connor, who had been talking to Matt, said, "You girls can take the next two days to catchup on any schoolwork, then depending on what the rangers say, we'll meet back at the mine on Monday morning."

Brenda said, "Great. I could work on my thesis a bit, adding in the work we've been doing here."

Tracy nodded. "I have plenty to keep me busy, also."

The four of them helped with the dinner cleanup, they liked to give Meg a break on nights they were out at the mine late. As the days got longer, they might end up out there late more often. The engineers took their leave to return to their own campers and cabin.

Once the kitchen was put to rights and the food was put away, they all trooped upstairs in a group. Inside Tracy's room, she and Brenda took seats on the bed, and Thomas took the desk chair. Lloyd remained standing, since he felt like he was the one to initiate this meeting it seemed appropriate.

Before he had a chance to speak, Tracy said, "I was thinking about something at dinner. I think Brenda and I need some new knowledge." Brenda looked intrigued but didn't interrupt and neither did he, so Tracy continued. "I think we need more knowledge on wildlife and what to do if we encounter it. I plan to look online to see what kind of information is out there, but you guys might already know where to look."

Lloyd grinned at her; it was exactly what he'd been thinking.

Tracy didn't acknowledge his grin but went on speaking, "And second, I think we need to learn about weapons." He knew the surprise lit his face. "At least the rifle. It's on the job site, but I don't know the first thing about handling it, even just to move it. Let alone if it became necessary to use the thing. I think Brenda and I both need to know how to use it."

Tracy turned toward Brenda. "We've chosen a career that puts us in the wilderness nearly full time. We need to know how to survive in it. We're two city girls, even a snake would scare the hell out of us, let alone a mountain lion or a bear. Please say you'll join me."

Brenda took Tracy's hand, "I'd be a fool not to. This possible wild cat encounter showed me how inadequate our experience is."

Tracy said, "Good. Now Lloyd, what is it you wanted to talk about?"

He grinned at Tracy. "You covered it perfectly, you even went farther than I had thought to go. Thomas and I can teach you gun safety and even how to shoot. Everyone on the ranch is required to have passed the gun safety certification. Thomas and I are even authorized to teach it."

"Yay, that makes the second part easier, I thought it would be the hard part."

Lloyd wanted to kiss her for her enthusiasm, but that could wait for later.

TRACY WAS SO EXCITED THAT HER THOUGHTS AND IDEAS HAD been met with positivity. She'd been worried they would laugh at her or even worse ignore her. But it seemed the other three were taking her seriously. It was a heady sensation.

Thomas nodded. "The best place to start on wildlife is the Colorado Park and Wildlife website. They have short articles on each species you should be familiar with in Colorado, and what to do if you encounter them."

Tracy typed that into her phone and their website popped up. She didn't want to read it now, but she saved it as a favorite. As she put her phone down, she noticed Brenda had done the same.

"Thanks, I'll look that over tomorrow. Now about the gun safety and shooting class."

Lloyd said, "I'll talk to Travis about it, let him know what we have in mind. We've got a small shooting range out behind the bunkhouse we can use.'

"Why don't you ladies plan to work on your schoolwork tomorrow," Thomas said, "We'll get everything set up and we can get started on Friday. By the way, during my tracking training I was taught how to find each animal in its natural habitat, so I've seen them all. Other than that, I think I've seen a bear twice and a cougar once. It's not normal to run into them often, unless you leave food out or do something else stupid. So, there is no need to worry, but knowledge is always good to have."

Lloyd agreed, "That would give us time to let everyone know what's going to be taking place, so no one worries about the sound."

Tracy was so excited. She wasn't a big gun fan but the fact she'd wished she knew more about them twice now indicated it was time to learn. Being helpless in the face of danger was not fun. "Thanks, guys. I think that would be perfect."

Brenda hugged her before she left. "Great ideas, Trace. We do need to know these things in our chosen profession. It's a wonder they don't have anything like this on campus."

"I was thinking the same thing. I may talk about it to Dr. Patricia tomorrow when we do our weekly mentorship call."

"Perfect."

When Brenda and Thomas had gone, Tracy was swept up into a huge hug by Lloyd, he lifted her off her feet and twirled her around.

She laughed. "What's gotten into you?"

He set her down and kissed her firmly. "There is just something incredibly sexy about a strong woman who isn't afraid to go after what she wants."

She poked him in the belly. "Is this because I agreed with you?"

He grabbed her finger and kissed the tip. "That might be a small part of it, but not all of it. You knew what you needed, and wanted to learn, and went about obtaining it. Even if it's not a girl kind of thing to do."

She laughed. "You do know I'm going to an engineering school where ninety percent of the student body is male, right? I think in the graduate program that percentage increases."

"Yeah, you've mentioned the mostly male environment, but I still find a woman that knows her own mind to be sexy as hell."

She was flying high on his compliments and her accomplishments. It was entirely gratifying to have a man think so highly of her. She teased him, "Maybe it's just me that's sexy."

"Oh, there's no doubt about that, but this takes it to a whole other level."

"Good, then you should show me."

"I was going to go talk to Travis."

"Since we're not starting until Friday, can't you talk to him tomorrow?" She ran her hand down his chest until it reached his belt buckle which she toyed with.

He swallowed loudly. "Sure, it can wait until tomorrow."

Tracy enjoyed the power she had over this strong man. Sometimes being a woman had its perks, having a man helpless in the face of her feminine abilities was definitely one of them. She was going to keep him on the edge for a while, she wanted to see how far she could push him before he lost his careful control.

She slowly undressed him. Kissing and licking every inch of skin she uncovered. He tried to remove her clothes, but she shook her head. "I get to be in control this time. You're just going to have to take what I give you."

He groaned. "If you insist."

"I do. I have this big male cowboy body to explore and it's going to take a long time."

"Are you trying to kill me?"

"Not at all, just testing your control a little." She smiled to herself knowing she planned to test his control a whole lot more than a little, but he didn't need to know that, yet.

When she had him down to his boxers and had kissed every bare inch of skin, she had him lay down on the bed and told him not to move his hands from where she'd placed them above his head. She'd deliberately avoided any contact with his straining cock. Making it wait. She had plans and the anticipation was definitely going to heighten the experience, for both of them.

She kissed his mouth for long drugging moments, not letting any other body part touch his. It was torment for both of them. She finally moved off the bed and did a slow strip tease while he watched avidly.

She ran her hands over her breasts pinching her nipples. His watching her, heightened the sensations she was feeling. She ran her hands down her torso, one hand slipping between her thighs. "I'm so wet for you, Lloyd."

He growled something she couldn't quite make out. His cock was creating quite an enormous tent and she decided it was time to play with that body part. She removed his boxers and licked her lips at the sight of what she'd done to him.

She bent down to give his cock a kiss and Lloyd ground out. "Oh no, you don't."

He grabbed her by the waist and positioned her above him. She supposed her teasing was over, so she let him impale her and it felt wonderful. She started to move on him slowly, but he was having none of it. When she didn't move fast enough for him, he flipped them over and took her on a wild ride to ecstasy. She didn't mind one bit that he'd taken control, in fact she marveled at his patience. She'd thought he would snap much sooner than he did.

When they lay together in a sweaty heap, he said, "I couldn't hold back any longer."

She mustered the energy to pat his chest. "You did just fine and I'm not complaining."

"Good. I plan to pay you back for all that torment, you know."

She laughed. "Soon I hope."

He chuckled and pulled the blankets up over the top of them. "Soon, but not quite yet, sleep, my wild cat."

She snuggled into him and did as he said. Paybacks could wait until they had enough energy to move.

CHAPTER 20

"Gun safety class is now in session," Thomas said.

Lloyd thought the comment was rather ridiculous, the four of them, Tracy, Brenda, Thomas and he were in a room where they had two tables set up. Each table had a shotgun, a rifle, and a handgun on them, plus gun cleaning supplies. When Lloyd had talked to Travis about teaching the girls how to shoot and handle the guns properly, Travis had suggested showing the ladies how to handle a smaller gun also.

"Those girls aren't going to be carrying around a shotgun or rifle in the field, but a handgun can be just as effective and is easier to carry. I taught Emma how to use a revolver for that very reason." Travis shrugged, "If she's on her horse it's easy to slip a shotgun or rifle into the scabbard, but for hiking or working in the field like the girls will be doing they'd have to carry it on their back. A pistol could fit in their pack or in a hip holster."

"They'd need to get a concealed carry permit to have it in their pack."

"Yeah, perfectly justifiable for anyone who works in the

128

wilderness like they will be. I'd bet Connor and Matt might have something on them, if not a gun, then a knife. Which might also be something you could teach them to use."

He'd told Thomas what Travis had recommended and Thomas had agreed with the plan, so now the girls were going to learn how to handle and shoot all three guns, safely and confidently.

Brenda asked. "Why do we have two shotguns?"

Thomas answered, "You don't. You have a shotgun and a rifle. A shotgun shoots a bunch of little beads, a rifle shoots a single bullet. They are similar in shape but not in what they shoot. Shotguns do not kill as easily, you have to be really close to kill with one. But they do sting and can cause an animal to go the other way. Rifles shoot bullets and make a hole, just like a handgun does, killing is likely or guaranteed, depending on where you hit."

Thomas began working with Brenda and Lloyd began working with Tracy. Tracy learned quickly and didn't seem hesitant about handling the weapons.

She said, "They are heavier than I expected."

"Yeah, most people say that, but after you've handled them for a while, you'll get used to their weight. We'll spend today's lesson working on safe handling, breaking them down, cleaning them, putting them back together and how to load them with the safety on."

"No shooting?"

"Nope, not until you are confident and capable doing all the rest. With the weight and learning all three weapons you'll probably be weary from handling them."

TRACY WAS DISAPPOINTED THEY WOULDN'T BE FIRING THE weapons today. She'd psyched herself up for it. She wasn't a gun fan, in fact they scared her, but this was something she needed to know to feel safe during field work, so she was determined to learn it.

Three guns for her to learn was more than she'd expected, but after Thomas had answered the question Brenda had asked, and which had been on Tracy's mind too, she understood. Lloyd had already told her about his conversation with Travis, so she'd known to expect to have a pistol in the mix.

She worked hard with Lloyd learning about the guns. He started with how to check to make sure the safety was on and how to hold and handle the weapon. Then he taught her the gun parts and explained what each was for, starting with the shotgun, then moving to the rifle, and lastly the handgun.

Taking apart each weapon showed her how each one had similar and different parts. Lloyd showed her how to carefully clean and oil each piece before putting them back together again. He had her practice over and over before moving on to the next weapon.

When they finally got to the loading of each one with ammunition, she was glad they were nearly done, her arms and hands hurt from the weight.

Lloyd said, "You've done well. Now let's test your knowledge. Give me fifteen minutes then come back for your test."

Brenda joined Tracy as she left the room.

"I had no idea this was going to be so exhausting," Brenda said rubbing her hands and arms.

"Yeah, when Lloyd said we wouldn't be shooting them I was disappointed, but now I'm glad. I'm not sure I have enough strength left to even lift them let alone fire one of them. It would probably knock me on my ass."

"You and me both, sister. I think we've got time for a potty break and to hit the kitchen for a snack."

Tracy grinned. "Perfect plan."

In the kitchen they each took a piece of fruit from the large bowl that always sat on the counter tempting passersby to grab a piece. Tracy chomped into her apple while Brenda quickly peeled the skin off a tangerine.

"I feel sorry for the guys not getting a break, they've been in there with us the whole time," Tracy said.

"Let's take them a snack then."

"Just a small one, we're not supposed to have food near the guns when they're open."

Brenda said, "They were all in one piece when we left. Why would they take them apart again?"

"For our quiz."

"Oh, don't be such a worry wart. We'll just cut up some fruit and keep it by the door for them to snack on."

Tracy wasn't sure this was a great idea, but she went along with it. They made a pretty fruit tray to take back with them.

When they started in the door, Thomas barked out, "You're late."

Brenda frowned and held out the fruit tray, we made you a snack. Tracy held paper plates and napkins.

"Have you lost your minds? Get that out of here." Thomas hollered. "No food or drinks around the guns."

Brenda spun around and Tracy followed her.

Thomas yelled out, "Both of you wash your hands and get back in here. We're not done."

Brenda said, "I'm not going back to be yelled at by that asshole."

Tracy guessed that Brenda had never been yelled at before. Her family was not in the least demonstrative, positively or negatively. They were cold formal people. Tracy couldn't imagine a raised voice.

"Brenda, no. He's just worried about the guns. We shouldn't have taken them food; they already told us never to have food around the guns."

Brenda's breath hitched, as she set the fruit plate on the kitchen counter. "He didn't have to yell at us."

Tracy hugged her friend. "Some people consider that a normal tone of voice."

"Well, I don't. It scared me and pissed me off."

"Come on, let's wash our hands and go back. You will probably need to talk to Thomas about his tone and volume."

Brenda gave her friend a watery smile. "You're probably right."

They left their fruit tray in the kitchen and scrubbed their hands in the sink before going back to the room they'd been using.

Lloyd and Thomas were nearly toe to toe with Lloyd speaking quietly to Thomas. When the girls entered Thomas glanced over, then nodded to Lloyd.

Thomas said, "I'm sorry I yelled. It's just that we told you —"

Lloyd cut him off as the volume had started to increase. "It was nice of you ladies to think of us, we could use a snack. We just can't let any contamination near the weapons, it could be dangerous to the next person to use them. Did you thoroughly wash your hands? Sticky fruit juice can be a real problem. Citrus can eat through the oil to possibly cause a jam. Other sticky fruit juice can be just as dangerous."

Brenda had her head down in shame. "We're sorry, we were just trying to be nice."

Tracy looked directly at Thomas. "She's never been

yelled at. You could have explained without raising your voice."

"I didn't yell."

Tracy and Lloyd said in unison, "Yes, you did."

Brenda looked up with tear-filled eyes and Thomas melted at the look. He took Brenda's hand and led her out of the room.

Tracy and Lloyd sat at their table. Lloyd whispered, "Tears can be just as bad as fruit juice."

Tracy smiled at him. "Thanks for taking control."

"No problem, I knew it would devastate her. I didn't know how you would take it."

She shrugged, "I've been in a yelling house or two." She hadn't liked it, but she'd learned to cope with it. Sometimes quiet was more scary than loud. Coping skills were something Tracy had in abundance.

"He had no idea. Thomas only uses that tone of voice when he's worried or upset."

She nodded. "Now why are all the gun pieces scattered on the table?"

"We want to check to see if you can determine one from another. Can you put the three guns back together?"

She looked back at the table. "Absolutely, can I start in any order?"

"Yes."

She started with the handgun, the more table space she could make the easier it would be to put the larger guns together. About the time she'd finished with the pistol, Thomas and Brenda entered the room. They both looked composed, still a little stressed out, but calm.

Tracy was glad to see them return, but she was ready to be done with the guns for today. She quickly put the last two together.

Lloyd said, "Excellent. Ready to get out of here?"

"So ready, can we go for a walk outside. Being in this room all day…" She trailed off.

Lloyd said, "Let me put the guns away. I'll meet you in the kitchen. I hope some of the fruit is still there."

Tracy picked up the pistol. "Show me where they go."

CHAPTER 21

*A*fter a stop by the kitchen to grab some of the fruit snacks, Tracy and Lloyd pulled on boots and jackets and went out into the chilly afternoon sunshine. She dragged in a deep breath of the bracing air and sighed in contentment.

Lloyd said, "You did good in there. I know it made for a long day, but it's the most critical part of handling weapons. Learning to shoot is mostly muscle, learning the weapon is knowledge, until it becomes rote. You want it to become rote, but rote that you take care paying attention to."

"I won't take a gun for granted. They still scare me a little."

"A gun in the hand of a novice should always scare you. It's not the equipment but the person whose hand it's in that is the real danger."

"But that same hand holding something less lethal is not as scary."

"I can't argue with you. A gun is made to kill, no getting around it."

She frowned at that statement; it was not quite the message she had received. "Even a shotgun?"

"On smaller game, yes. Birds, squirrels, things like that."

"Oh, you made it sound safe."

"For a cougar or a bear, yeah, it'll sting, not kill them. But it's still propelling little pieces of metal at a high rate of speed. The big animals have thick skin that protects them from the shot."

They walked for a while in silence, Tracy turned over in her head all she'd learned today.

Lloyd interrupted her thoughts. "Is Brenda going to be able to forgive Thomas for yelling?"

"I think so, but he'll have to learn that shouting is not the most effective way to work with Brenda. She had a very silent and cold family, so heated emotion and noise is far outside her ability to handle."

"Have you met her parents?"

"Yes, both of them, and that one time each was more than enough. They aren't married any more, but I got the same chills meeting one as I did the other. They barely acknowledge Brenda; they are the only thing important to themselves. It was kind of creepy."

"Considering your upbringing I can't imagine what it would feel like to someone, like Thomas, from a loving family."

Tracy laughed at Lloyd's expression. "They'd probably be shocked. Heck, I was shocked. When we finally got away from them, I felt kind of frozen. It took Brenda and I a while to get back to normal."

"I hope I never have the 'pleasure' of meeting them." Tracy noticed from Lloyd's tone of voice that the word pleasure had air quotes around it.

"I hope that too, for your sake."

❧

LLOYD FOUND IT HARD TO BELIEVE BRENDA'S PARENTS WERE so odd, but one thing he'd learned about Tracy, she never exaggerated, and she never sugar-coated. What she said was an accurate presentation of facts. Always.

"Are you looking forward to shooting tomorrow?"

"I am, but I'm glad we didn't try to do it today. My hands hurt and my arms feel like Jell-O from hoisting all that heavy metal."

He could help with the first one. He stopped walking and turned toward her, taking her right hand he firmly massaged it. "When we get back to the house, we'll do this again with cream made to help tired muscles."

"It already feels better."

"Good." Her hands were small but strong, so for her to admit they hurt he knew they had probably overdone it a bit today. Normally they didn't work with multiple fire-arms at the same time.

When her skin was reddened and warm, he switched hands.

She flexed the one he'd worked on. "It feels so much better, thanks."

"You're welcome, after dinner when you can strip down to just a sports bra, I'll give your arms and shoulders a massage too."

She grinned up at him. "Is that a euphemism for…"

"No. I plan to help your muscles feel better."

Her shoulders slumped and she pouted. "Bummer."

He laughed, she delighted him. "Of course, after your massage, if you get frisky, I'm not going to fight you off."

"Oh, goody, well prepare to meet my frisky side."

He thought back to their previous encounters. "You mean I haven't already?"

"Nope. I've been holding back."

He sighed with a large amount of exaggeration. "If we must, I will bow to your enthusiasm. I just hope I can keep up."

She laughed and jumped up grabbing his hair and wrapping her legs around his waist, she pulled his head down to hers and laid a steamy kiss on his lips.

He was so caught up in the kiss that he jumped, nearly dropping her when a cow mooed next to him. He looked down to find Dolly, the old heifer Beau had saved as a kid, who was now the ranch mascot. She was far past childbearing age and should have been dealt with, but instead she roamed the ranch freely.

He said to the cow. "So do you approve?"

Tracy laughed when the cow nodded her head. Or at least it appeared that she'd nodded.

He said, "Glad we could be of service."

Tracy slid down from her perch. "It's probably time we were moseying on back."

A laugh burst forth. "Moseying? Where did you pick that up, city girl?"

She winked at him and started back toward the house.

Dolly let out another long moo, that sounded like laughter.

He shot Dolly a look and then followed after the girl.

CHAPTER 22

The days got warmer and longer as they moved into spring. There was no more trouble at the mine, they continued to work toward being able to cover the tailing area with a thick layer of soil that would be delivered soon, then they would plant trees and bushes to put the contamination far below the growth or any weather.

They took a couple of short trips during the girls' spring break from school, one to Glenwood Springs to play in the hot springs and another to Central City to throw money away in the casinos. But the rest of the time they just worked like normal.

Tracy had been very conservative in the casinos; she didn't like just tossing money away and she knew too much math to ignore the ridiculous odds of actually winning. This was the first time in her life that she had a decent income, and she wasn't about to waste it on gambling.

Brenda had talked her into it, so she'd taken her sixty dollars and had gone along. She played small and never let herself lose more than what she'd set aside. She'd been surprised that she'd won little bits that had allowed her to keep playing long after she'd thought she would have. But she supposed that was the strategy, if a player only lost, they would eventually stop playing.

Tracy had tried the slots and then went to each different table to see how the games were played, it had been a learning experience and she'd ended up with twenty dollars, only losing forty so she was happy with the outcome.

Brenda sighed on the way back from the casino. "I had so much fun, I lost more than I won, but that's how the casinos stay in business."

Tracy smiled at her friend. She knew Brenda had as much math knowledge as she did so wasn't at all surprised. "It was fun, I won just often enough to keep me playing. I still have twenty dollars."

Lloyd, who was the navigator and also lookout, glanced back for just a moment. "You're the lucky one then. They got five more dollars out of me than what I'd intended on."

Thomas chuckled, "Brenda's enthusiasm got the better of me, I lost about fifty more than I'd intended."

Lloyd pointed out something on the side of the road and Thomas slowed. It was a raccoon family. Tracy was charmed by them but glad they stayed on the shoulder rather than venturing into the road. Once they were safely past the small group Thomas picked up the pace.

Tracy now understood the lookout role Lloyd was fulfilling, it was a lookout for nocturnal animals. Thomas didn't need a navigator, both men knew the roads, but a second set of eyes looking for critters was an excellent plan.

Tracy stayed alert watching for any trouble. Brenda, on the other hand, passed out before they got back to the interstate. Once they hit the interstate Tracy relaxed enough to fall asleep too.

LLOYD GLANCED BACK TO SEE BOTH GIRLS WERE ASLEEP. HE spoke low to Thomas, "Ladies are out."

"Easier to concentrate that way."

"Brenda seemed to have a wonderful time," Lloyd said.

"She did, thanks for coming along."

"Tracy and I enjoyed ourselves too."

"I know. Tracy wasn't all that excited about the idea in the beginning."

"Wasting money is hard for her."

Thomas nodded. "Yeah, that's one thing I never really had to worry about. I've been part of the Rockin' K my whole life and they pay well, most of my salary is in the bank."

"Yeah, right there with you, once my dad lost the gold fever."

Thomas frowned. "I can't figure out why things have been so quiet lately. We had trouble for a couple of months and since then, nothing. Sometimes the cameras are pointed off in random directions, but I can't say they've been tampered with."

"Yeah, I agree. I keep wondering if the other shoe is going to drop one of these days."

"We just keep our eyes and ears open and be ready to take action," Thomas said.

"Agreed."

Thomas said, "Did you hear that Jen from the café is seeing some guy?"

"Yeah, that new forest ranger."

"The one with a southern accent?"

"Yep, only new ranger we've gotten in years."

Thomas chuckled, "Guess that's true. I hope he's good to her."

"Gotta be, southern gentleman and all that."

Thomas glanced over. "That and she'd kick his ass if he wasn't decent."

Lloyd had to agree with that, Jen didn't take shit from anyone. Hadn't in years. "True."

They turned off the interstate and they both went back to careful observation; animals could be a problem on these smaller roads. It didn't pay to be chatting and not paying attention, one buck could total a vehicle.

RAY LAY BACK ON HIS BED, CONTENT WITH HIS LIFE. HE'D planned to hightail it back to Georgia the moment Buddy was ready to leave, but now he was rethinking that idea. He was enjoying Jennifer, at least he assumed her full name was Jennifer, she went by Jen at work, they'd never discussed it. She was a sweet girl and they enjoyed each other's company.

She wasn't clingy and was fine with him sleeping in his own bed, even after a night of tearing up the sheets together. He enjoyed spending the night with her, except on workdays, she had to get up so darn early and he was a light sleeper, so he usually slept at the cabin on her workdays.

They could talk for hours or enjoy silence. Their movie preferences were similar, and they both enjoyed a cold beer after a long workday. They'd become regulars at the bar in town, or he had, she'd already been one.

They avoided karaoke night at the bar like the plague. She hated the offkey singing as much as he did. Those nights they spent in her small place above one of the tourist shops, a six pack of beer and a movie on one of the channels and they were happy as could be.

Buddy had finally gotten over his schemes to get rid of

the engineers cleaning up the mine tailings. Once Ray had found out that the plan was just to cover the tailing area not the whole place Buddy had calmed down. No one in their right mind would bury anything under that mess.

So now all they did was go down on weekends and continue their hunt. It was easy to move the cameras just enough that their work area wasn't showing. Plus, Ray thought that maybe Buddy had found a skirt in one of the outlying towns, because he was spending a lot of time away from the cabin and was clean, with his laundry done more often. Buddy was rarely home when Ray got off work.

So, everything had settled on a nice track. Life was pretty darn good, even though he did miss the swamps of home and the heat. The cold still got into his bones sometimes. But he could be happy here.

He still had his and his mother's homes in Georgia and he wondered if he should put them up for sale. That seemed like a big step, so he would put that off until they found the gold. If they ever did. He was beginning to believe that the stories of fortune were simply tales told to children to fire their imagination. Nothing more. He couldn't convince Buddy of that though, so they continued to dig on weekends.

Buddy drove slowly on the road back to Spirit Lake, cursing himself for not staying, he'd had one too many to be driving. Karla had invited him to stay but he was getting tired of her and her whiny ways. She didn't like it when he played cards with the guys he'd met, suckers every one of them.

He was robbing them blind with his country boy drawl and blank expressions. He knew how to cheat and then look surprised as he raked in the pot. Karla had no idea that playing cards with the boys is what kept him in beer money, with a few dollars to take her out once in a while or order a pizza in.

Thank fuck she was a modern woman and insisted on paying over half the time. And she gave good head, and was eager to spread her legs for him. Her only real fault was wanting to cuddle while they slept. God, he hated a broad wrapped around him all night, like a fucking python squeezing the air out of him.

So, to avoid that again tonight, he was blearily driving back to the cabin he shared with his brother. Just a few more miles. He rolled down the windows to let the cold air in to keep him alert and popped a breath mint in his mouth.

As the miles passed, he contemplated other ways to get those nosy engineers out of his way. He was tired of this cold damn country and wanted to get back to Georgia. He needed to find the gold and be done with it.

His brother thought he'd given up on his plans to move the engineers along. He was wrong about that, but Buddy hadn't come up with a fool proof way yet and he'd made enough mistakes that everyone was keeping a close eye on things. It needed to look natural, even to those snoopy rangers and the cowboys who'd lived here all their lives.

Too bad they didn't have tornados or hurricanes; he knew how to capitalize on those. They had pretty strong wind, hail, and thunderstorms. How could he use those elements? There had to be a way.

CHAPTER 23

*T*racy hadn't talked to her mentor, Patricia, in weeks. The baby had given Patricia some trouble toward the end of her pregnancy that had kept her out of the office, so she'd missed several weekly mentorship calls.

She'd had a beautiful baby girl they'd named Amelia, such a pretty name. Dr. Patricia was finally back in the office with baby Amelia by her side. Graduation was in a few weeks and also the end of the semester, so Patricia had had no choice but to get back to her office.

Tracy had a list of things she needed or wanted to talk to her mentor about. She knew Brenda was feeling even more pressure since Steve had taken time off for the baby and to support Patricia, and Brenda was graduating and needed to wrap everything up.

As Tracy waited for Patricia to join the online call, she checked her list of topics one more time.

Patricia came online with Amelia on her shoulder as she patted the baby's back. "Sorry I'm late. She had to eat and was taking her sweet time."

Tracy said, "Babies don't care about schedules, at least not any but their own."

The mother's smile said it all, all kinds of love poured across the airways and Tracy wondered if her mother had been the same, before the accident that had left her an orphan. "She's amazing. I can't wait to see her at graduation."

"Speaking of which, we've got a lot to talk about. The semester end is right around the corner. Let's get to it."

They talked about all the requirements that needed to be finalized in the next few weeks. Tracy took notes on the conversation, highlighting 'to do' items, especially the things she hadn't thought of earlier.

Patricia said, "It sounds like you've got things well in hand. Send me the draft of your thesis so I can see if you need to be redirected anywhere."

"I'll do that. I have one other thing I want to run past you. Do you have a few more minutes?"

"Absolutely, go ahead."

"I think there are a couple of pieces missing from our education."

Patricia's eyebrows rose, but she let Tracy go on.

Tracy explained about the wild animals and how she and Brenda, as city girls, had no idea what to do about the various species they might bump into out in the wilderness. She told her mentor about the gun safety and shooting class the guys had designed for them. "I think other students might benefit by some similar classes, or maybe an after-school club to prepare them for the field."

"You bring up some good points. The wildlife subject would be good, but not everyone is going to end up in the Colorado mountains, some of them are going to end up in the coastal regions where swamp conditions bring entirely different species to learn about. I'm not sure how that would work, but I'll talk it over with Steve and some of the other professors to see if we can come up with an idea."

Tracy hadn't thought about other areas, other states and different wildlife, but that was why Patricia was the mentor and she was the mentee. "That would be great."

"The gun safety and possible shooting practice would be more generic, but would take some official coordination. Just anybody can't teach those things, even in an informal after school club. There would need to be a certified instructor. I don't know about insurance regulations and things like that. There might be a way to take the students to an official gun range. Lots of things to think about and investigate. But worth looking into, we don't want our students going out unprepared for dealing with whatever they might come up against."

"I guess Brenda and I were lucky to have certified people on the ranch and the private insurance to cover the training."

"You were, but that doesn't mean we'll just set this issue aside. That's what we have staff meetings for, to discuss where we think something might be missing from your education."

"Thanks, Dr. Patricia. I'll get started on the list I made and see you and baby Amelia in person soon."

"I'm looking forward to it."

LLOYD WAS UP AT THE MINE WORKING WITH MATT, HIS LEAST favorite guy to work with, simply because he never quite knew when Matt was going to bring up getting certified again. Matt was intelligent and Lloyd always learned a lot when he worked with him, but waiting for Matt to bug him about school made Lloyd tense.

He'd looked into the programs and considered taking a look at the school when they all went for Brenda's graduation in a few weeks, but he was still leaning toward staying on the ranch where he belonged.

Maybe it was cowardice to not want to chance being rejected out in the 'real' world. He knew his place on the ranch and everyone understood his disability and they'd come up with a solution for it. Lloyd always worked with a partner whose job was to verify any records Lloyd touched. He was comfortable with that, but to go off to a school of higher education, even just a one-year certification course, where he'd have to do everything aurally and be exposed as barely able to read, he wasn't at all comfortable with that idea.

He rationally told himself if wouldn't be like public education or being a kid, but those arguments didn't stop the trepidation he felt when he gave the idea any credence. He needed to stop thinking about it, he wasn't going and that was final.

Matt kept working his eyes never leaving his task when he said, "You know the certification class is really small, less than a dozen students per year."

Dammit, had he said something out loud, or was Matt becoming a mind reader? Lloyd didn't answer, just kept working.

"Steve is one of the instructors, you already know him."

Again, Lloyd ignored the man.

"It's on the other side of town from the college, but close enough to get an apartment with Tracy."

He groaned. "Matt, leave it."

"You should at least go by and check it out when you go to Grandville for Brenda's graduation."

"If I promise to go by and see it, will you shut the hell up about it?"

Lloyd could see the grin on Matt's face, even as he tried to hide it. "Sure."

"Fine, Tracy and I will check it out."

Matt didn't answer, but Lloyd could practically feel the man jump up and click his heels together.

CHAPTER 24

*T*he drive to the college was filled with chatter. Brenda had gotten news that her parents would both be attending the ceremony. Brenda had been certain they wouldn't trouble themselves to show up.

Brenda babbled, "Thank goodness I didn't throw my parents' tickets in the trash. It never occurred to me they would actually show up. When the school sent me eight tickets, I figured only the three for you guys would be used. I thought about inviting Travis, Meg, and Grandpa K, but figured that was being too needy. Good thing I didn't. Now, I'll only have one extra instead of five."

Tracy decided only an outrageous remark would give Brenda respite from saying the same thing over and over. "Maybe one of your parents is into menage this week and you can use the last one."

Brenda laughed. "Wouldn't that be the kicker. But no, my parents are too respectable to do something so extreme."

Tracy said, "I might pay money to see something like that from your parents."

"Me too. Will you sit with them, Thomas?"

"If you want me to."

"Yes, please. That lets you and Lloyd off the hook," she said to Tracy.

"Excellent."

Lloyd said, "While you get pictures taken and are hugged by all the other students, Tracy and I are going to go by the Reclamation certification school. I promised Matt."

Brenda looked back through the seats to Lloyd. "Does that mean you're thinking ab—"

"Attending? Nope, but Matt was bugging me, so I promised to check it out while we were in town. It got him to shut the hell up."

"Oh, for what it's worth, I think you'd do very well."

"Thanks, but I'm not interested."

Tracy decided to change the subject. "I'm so glad they're having commencement outdoors this year, I know it's harder to set up all the seats, but I still prefer it to indoors. Especially on a pretty day like today."

Brenda said, "I agree. Plus, when the speeches get boring you can look at trees and stuff instead of walls."

Lloyd asked, "But I'll bet the acoustics are worse, aren't they?"

"All the better to ignore the boring speeches," Tracy said with a grin.

Lloyd shook his head. "I see you're not a fan of the speeches."

"After sitting through hundreds of hours of lectures, graduation speeches are at the bottom of my list of things I want to do." Tracy linked her fingers with his. "You'll be ready to run, trust me."

"You never know, I might be an avid fan."

❦

WHAT SEEMED LIKE HOURS LATER, LLOYD COULD ADMIT HE was not an avid fan. When Brenda finally walked across the stage, he heard Thomas let out a whoop. He and Tracy escaped shortly after that, going back to where they'd parked the truck and driving it across town to see the certification school. It was in an older building behind a park. He wondered if it had been a campus at one time.

Tracy confirmed his thought when she said, "This used to be the old campus for the college, when it was just one subject."

"What one subject?"

"Mining, of course. Everything else came later. Colorado has always had mining, gold, silver, gems, coal, you name it, Colorado has it all."

"I've lived here all my life and didn't know that."

Tracy shrugged, "Why would you? It's not common knowledge unless it's been part of your life, or in my case, education."

They went into the school, the halls were quiet, and they wandered around a bit, looking in windows. There was a chemistry lab, a room with all kinds of equipment in it, some of it he recognized but a lot he didn't, there were several empty classrooms. They finally found one room with about ten students and a teacher giving a lecture.

It was a small class size, just as Matt had said. They went to the office last, where a cheerful woman met them. "Hello, how can I help you?"

Tracy took the lead and Lloyd let her because his throat had gone dry as the idea of attending was peeked.

"Someone we know suggested we stop in and have a look around. Do you have any information on attending the school?"

"Of course, we have this packet. There is only one

curriculum, and the classes are very small, but the certification is top notch. Which one of you is interested in attending?"

Tracy hedged, "We're just gathering information for now, nothing as formal as one of us attending."

Lloyd was glad she'd phrased it that way, he didn't want any attention directed at him.

Tracy's phone buzzed. "Oh, we need to go. Thanks for the information, we'll be in touch should we decide to pursue this."

The woman smiled, "Thanks for stopping by, do call or come back if you have any questions. If you don't mind, can you tell me who referred you?"

"Matt Sismour," Tracy said absently as she texted someone back.

That caught the woman's attention and she zeroed in on Lloyd. "Our curriculum is very open, and our instructors are willing and able to work with students one on one, as needed. I hope you give our program careful consideration."

Lloyd mumbled a thanks and hauled Tracy out the door, the packet of information clutched tightly in his hand. Matt had obviously talked to the woman and instructors about him, and he didn't like it one little bit.

As they got in the truck, he tossed the information into the back seat. Damn, he hated being the center of attention, especially when his reading disability caused it.

Tracy said, "The text was from Brenda, she wants us to meet her at the Mexican restaurant. Her parents must have bailed, she would never take them to our favorite dive."

Lloyd had the steering wheel in a death grip, he was glad Tracy was preoccupied with Brenda. "Tell me where to go."

By the time they found parking he'd calmed down enough to join the others. Tracy pointed out that Brenda and Thomas were at the front of the line, so they joined them.

Tracy sucked in a breath, "Have you been crying? Did your parents—"

Brenda's smile could have lit the entire town, the entire front range. "Happy tears." She held out her hand. "Thomas asked me to marry him, and I said yes."

Tracy squealed and crushed her in a hug. "I'm so happy for you."

"I'm happy for me, too."

While Tracy exclaimed over the ring, Lloyd slapped Thomas on the back. "Good job, bud." He thought Thomas looked a little stunned, Lloyd decided he needed to be his wing man, which allowed him to put the earlier encounter to the back of his mind.

He kissed Brenda's cheek, and they went into the restaurant where champagne was ordered, and it went just fine with the delicious Mexican food.

CHAPTER 25

*L*loyd glared at the packet of papers on the chest of drawers in his room. He'd not opened it since they got back from Grandville, three days ago. He knew he was being foolish, but he couldn't help himself. If he opened it and it looked great, he'd be tempted to go and then he'd end up being humiliated. On the other hand, if he opened it and it looked awful the tiny spark of interest would die and he'd go back to being just a ranch hand.

God he was a pathetic mess. He should just get it over with, but he didn't move toward the packet, he just glared at it from across the room. He knew Matt would corner him one of these days and demand a recounting, but he simply could not bring himself to open the packet. Matt would just have to wait, he'd already told the man no, in more ways than he could count.

A knock on his door pulled him out of his thoughts. He opened the door to Thomas.

"Let's go, dinner at the big house tonight, Tony's back in town for two days only."

Shit, he'd forgotten completely, at least he'd already

cleaned up after the day's work. Tony was one of his favorite people, so for him to forget, meant he was clearly out of his damn mind about those ridiculous papers. He was tempted to light them on fire. "Right behind you."

Dinner was a celebration, as each person walked into the dining room Tony came running to greet them.

"Mister Lloyd, I'm here, did you know I was here?"

Lloyd crouched down to Tony's height and shook hands with the little boy, which turned into a hug. "I heard a rumor you might be. How did you get so tall Tony? You are growing like a weed."

"It's all the good food mommy feeds me, mister Lloyd. Did you see the babies? They are very tiny and can't do anything yet, but Katie says they'll be more fun soon."

"I have seen the babies, but just one time. They haven't been born very long."

"A whole month, mister Lloyd. That seems like a long time to me."

"Naw, it's not long at all for a baby. They won't be able to walk for a whole year."

Tony's eyes got as big as saucers. "A whole year? Are you joshin' me, mister Lloyd?"

"Nope, that's how long it takes for them to grow strong enough."

"Wow." Tony ran off across the room to where Katie and Summer were holding court with the newborns. "Mister Lloyd said the babies won't be able to walk for a whole year.

Tracy linked arms with Lloyd. "Now you've done it. I think Tony thought they'd be all grown and ready to play with him when he gets off this year's rodeo circuit."

Lloyd chuckled. "Sorry to shatter his illusions."

"I don't think it will hold him down for long." Lloyd followed her gaze to where Tony was hopping on one foot and making faces to cause two-year-old Emily to howl with laughter.

"Nope, guess not."

The chaos was interrupted by Meg and her helpers carrying the food to the table.

When everyone was seated, the food was passed and the blessing said, Emma turned to Brenda, "I hear congratulations are in order on several fronts."

Brenda turned bright red as an enormous grin covered her face. "You're right, I am officially Dr. Brenda Stratton, but an even better name change will be when I become Mrs. Thomas Blackhawk." She held out her hand, so Emma could see the pretty engagement ring.

Emma exclaimed over it and looked up at Thomas, "You did good."

Now it was Thomas who turned red with a huge smile on his face.

Emma said, "So what did Dr. Patricia have? She was due in March, wasn't she?"

Tracy said, "She had a pretty baby girl that they named Amelia. She's got Steve's blue eyes and Patricia's blonde hair, at least it looks blonde now."

Emma asked, "Do you have pictures?"

Lloyd groaned. "Only about a hundred. Or maybe two hundred."

Tracy elbowed him as she handed her phone across the table to Emma. "There are only six or maybe ten."

Brenda said, "I have ten more."

After they had passed the phones around so everyone could see and coo over the pictures of Steve and Patricia's baby, the talk turned to the rodeo.

Emma said proudly, "Zach's in line to make All-Around cowboy this year."

Meg gasped, "Really? That's fantastic. Congratulations, Zach."

Zach shook his head. "It's way too soon for congratulations, a lot of the season is left, and hopefully Emma didn't just jinx me."

∾

Tracy didn't understand much about the rodeo circuit, so she tuned out much of the conversation about it.

When the subject started to wind down, Alyssa asked, "So if you win does that mean you'll be ready to give Tony a sibling?"

Emma's eyes widened, and she shook her head. "Not yet, we've got plenty of time to get around to more kids, I'm only twenty-six, plenty of time yet. Besides, rodeo is a young person's sport, so we gotta do it while we can, and since I'm half of the team roping, we aren't in any hurry."

Meg patted Emma's hand. "I think Alyssa was being her normal mischievous self. Let's turn it back on her, shall we? So, when will Emily be getting a sibling?"

Alyssa grinned like they had played right into her hands. "About November, I think."

The table erupted in joy. When all the delight died down Emma pointed at Alyssa. "That was sneaky."

Alyssa shrugged, an impish smile on her face. "One of my best traits."

Emma shook her head. "Poor Beau."

The whole table burst into laughter.

Tracy loved this family, they were so much fun, she hoped someday she could build a fun family like this one. She was the same age as Emma, who already had one child and a loving husband.

Tracy barely had a boyfriend in Lloyd, she wasn't even sure he counted as a boyfriend. They'd never talked about it. The fact that they were both living on the ranch in an enclosed environment meant they were exclusive as far as sleeping together and not dating anyone else. But was that just convenience? Sure, they liked one another, and they were good friends. Good friends with benefits, she supposed. Was that enough? She guessed it had to be, at least for now. In the fall, when she went back to campus, she had no idea what would happen.

Going back to campus without Brenda was something she was pushing to the far back of her thoughts. She didn't like any of the feelings she got when she thought about it, so she firmly *did not* think about it. She had three months before she had to, and she was going to enjoy every damn day of them.

CHAPTER 26

*L*loyd was in a hell of a shitty mood. He'd finally shoved those fucking papers into the bottom drawer of his chest under ratty clothes he never wore, but still they taunted him. He was just going to go work at the mine and ignore them. What he wanted to do was go out and work with the cattle, but no he was assigned to the engineers for the duration, dammit.

Being around the engineers made him think about the school, he'd even begged off from spending the night with Tracy. He'd come up with some lame excuse that she probably saw right through, but he'd just needed some space. Not that it'd done any good because the guys in the bunk house were having a rousing game of poker and were noisy as hell.

Normally he'd go out and join them, but his mood was too foul to impose it on the men he worked with, lived with, and liked. So, he'd sat in his room fuming and glaring at the damn drawer where the papers were, mocking him.

So, he'd probably hurt Tracy's feelings and it hadn't done a damn bit of good. Shit, he hated being so pissy, it went against his nature. He climbed in the truck next to Tracy and kind of grunted a hello, Thomas was driving with Brenda next to him in the front.

Tracy said, "It was fun seeing Tony last night, he's such a cute kid."

Brenda laughed. "And the way Beau and Alyssa suckered everyone in so they could make their baby announcement was great."

Even the talk of the family antics couldn't raise his spirits. He pulled out his phone to disengage from the people around him. He didn't want to say anything and was afraid if he did it would come out cranky. Offending them was not something he wanted to do.

Brenda and Tracy chattered on about the next steps at the mine. They'd determined that it was about time to start the planting phase. Which meant hauling a bunch of dirt and partially grown plants around. It would be a lot of hard work.

Tracy said, "I wonder when this Ramona is going to get here, since she seems to be the head of this next phase."

"Probably any day now. Connor said she has a little son, a bit younger than Tony. It's too bad Tony won't be around much; he probably would have enjoyed a younger playmate." Thomas said.

Brenda turned back toward Tracy. "I think it would be hard to raise a child on the road, especially alone. Being a single mother is hard enough without trying to do it in a trailer."

"Yeah, but didn't they say she pays one of her sisters to accompany them and take care of the little guy while Ramona works?"

Brenda nodded. "Since both of us are only children we have no idea what that would be like."

"True."

Lloyd heard Tracy's phone chime and she pulled it out of

her pocket. "Oh, Steve, Patricia, and baby Amelia are coming over for a few days, next week. They're bringing Steve's ex-brother-in-law, I guess he's going to help with the planting."

Brenda elbowed Thomas, "His name is Thomas, too. That should make things interesting."

"Well, he'll have to be Thomas two, or maybe he can go by Tom."

"Maybe, I've never heard Steve call him anything but Thomas."

"So, Steve is friendly with his ex-brother-in-law?" Thomas asked.

"Yeah, he's quite a bit younger and kind of looks up to Steve, the kid was orphaned in high school and Steve took them on." Brenda shrugged. "There's more to the story but I'm not up on all the deets."

They finally arrived at the cabin and Lloyd couldn't wait to get out of the truck. Maybe he could get put on the hauling detail and wouldn't have to be around people so much.

TRACY WONDERED WHAT WAS WRONG WITH LLOYD, HE'D BEEN quiet on the way out here and barely said a word. Just kind of grunted. He'd gone back to the bunkhouse last night after dinner, saying he had something he needed to do. She couldn't help but think that he was mad at her for some reason. She couldn't think of anything she'd done, but why else would he be surly?

She kept glancing at him, wondering if she should ask. Not in front of anyone, of course, he didn't like being put on the spot. They were taking the four-wheelers up now that the snow had melted, and the dirt was drying out. There were still some patches of mud, but nothing that couldn't be avoided.

They loaded up the four-wheelers and the trailers with the dirt that had been dumped in a large pile. It was heavy, sweaty work and she knew her muscles would ache later. Shoveling dirt was not part of her exercise routine, at least not until today. They filled all the trailers and hadn't even made a dent in the dirt.

She groaned inwardly, thinking about the days it would take them to move the dirt, let alone plant all the trees and shrubs to anchor that dirt. She climbed on the back of the four-wheeler with Lloyd, and they started up the hill.

Now was a good time to ask. "Did I do something to make you angry?"

"Nope."

"Are you sure?"

"Yep. Just got a lot on my mind."

Tracy wasn't sure she believed him, but she let the subject drop.

Lloyd barely stayed long enough to empty the trailer before he said, "I'll go back for another load."

Thomas and the two younger engineers all followed suit, while the other four of them started moving the dirt on top of the tailings.

By ten-thirty Tracy was exhausted and feeling cranky. She'd never worked so hard in her life. She had blisters on her hands, and her back was killing her. She slumped down on the ground next to Brenda who was guzzling water.

"They are trying to kill us," she said to her friend.

Brenda wiped her mouth and caused a dirt smear. "I agree. I had no idea when I signed up for this, that we'd be shoveling dirt."

"Me neither. I'm not a fan." Tracy dug her water bottle out and drank deeply.

Matt crouched down next to them. "Normally we can get a truck in closer to dump the dirt in a better position."

"We'll also get a crew in to do more of it tomorrow. We didn't think the dirt would be here today."

"Thank goodness. I'm not made for shoveling," Tracy said with a whimper.

Matt chuckled. "It'll put some meat on those bones." Then he sobered. "Don't overdo it. You girls are both little things, if it starts to give you severe pain just stop, we can get the work done."

They nodded as he stood and left them. Brenda lifted one eyebrow, "Did he just insinuate we couldn't handle the job because of our gender and size."

"Yep."

"Are we going to just stop and let the men handle it?"

"No way, we didn't go to an almost all male school to be the little women. Right?"

"No, we did not." Brenda stood with a moan. "Although, I'm tempted."

Tracy groaned as she stood. "Come on let's show these guys what we're made of."

CHAPTER 27

*D*amn he hurt all over, who knew that hauling dirt was such hard work, it wasn't even noon, and he was covered in sweat, and dirt clung to every inch of him. He'd worked off most of his mad, which was a good thing.

He got back to the mine with his newest batch of dirt. Tracy met him, she was a mess, her clothes were covered in dirt, there was a smear of it on her cheeks which were bright red, she was breathing heavily, her hair was falling out of the ponytail she had it in, and if he wasn't seeing things, her hands were covered in blisters, some of which had broken and were bleeding.

"Hey, you need to take it easy." He grabbed her hand; he was right, some blisters had popped. "You need to take care of these blisters. Where are your gloves?"

"The gloves caused the damn blisters in the first place; they don't fit quite right."

"You still need to take care of these they can become infected. And you're breathing so hard I'm worried you might have a heart attack. Now sit down over there and let me get the first aid kit."

"I don't need tending to, by the big strong man. I can handle this work just like you can."

He didn't answer, just pushed her down and went to get the first aid kit. He noticed Thomas was speaking to Brenda and handing her a bottle of water. She looked just as bad as Tracy did, what were these girls trying to prove?

He got the first aid kit and three bottles of water, two for them to drink and one to rinse the dirt and blood off Tracy's hands. He set the bottles down and started working on her hands. What he saw pissed him off.

In a low voice he said, "Just what are you girls trying to prove by working so hard?"

"That we can do the same job as a man, thank you very much."

He glanced around at the men, who were covered in dirt and sweat but their faces were not bright red and their hands weren't bleeding. "I think you're going about it the wrong way, look at the guys, none of them are as worn out as you and Brenda. You two are working yourselves too hard."

She glared at him and then turned her face away. "We are not."

"You are." He took her chin and forced her to look at the others. "Their faces aren't red. Their hands aren't bleeding. They are working but not killing themselves. Why are you?"

"Because Matt said we were so little that we shouldn't work too hard. It pissed us off."

His anger roared. "That's the stupidest thing I've ever heard. Both of you are a good six inches shorter than everyone of us guys. Your hands are smaller, which is probably why the gloves don't fit and caused the blisters. Why in the holy hell would him pointing that out make you act like a damn fool?"

Tracy's eyes narrowed. "You wouldn't understand because you're a man."

"So now you're calling me misogynistic?"

"If the shoe fits."

He wanted to shake some sense into her, but clamped his jaw shut and cleaned and bandaged her hands.

"I can't work like this," she said.

"No, you can't. I'm taking you back to the house, you're done for the day."

"You aren't in control of me. You're not my boss or my mom. You're not even officially my boyfriend, just someone to have sex with when you feel like it."

That hurt, but instead of letting her see it, he said, "Thank God for that."

She folded her arms across her chest. "Besides you haven't been mister sunshine yourself."

"I'm working through some things that have nothing to do with you."

She flinched like he'd slapped her, but what he'd said was true, she had nothing to do with his choices. She would be leaving at the end of the summer. Fuck it.

He took the first aid kit back to the cave and told Connor he was taking Tracy back to the house, that her hands were torn up from ill-fitting gloves. He marched over and unhooked the trailer full of dirt then pointed at Tracy to get on the back.

When they got back to the ranch house Tracy leaped off the back and was inside the house before he even got the four-wheeler parked.

Grandpa K came out of the barn. "What's up?"

"Tracy tore up her hands shoveling dirt, so I wrapped them and brought her back. She didn't like my interference;

she and Brenda seem to think they have to prove they are men in women's bodies."

Grandpa K leaned back on his heels. "Strong women sometimes need to learn what that means. They'll both figure it out eventually. But I sense something else is going on with you, son. I'm ready to listen if you want to talk about it."

"Oh, it's just that damn school Matt wants me to attend, we went by there after Brenda's graduation. They gave me a fucking packet of information about the school. To read."

"Ah."

"I'm sure I could muddle through it enough to get the drift, or have someone read it to me. But that's the reason for my resistance in the first place, I can't read. How many other things will be like that?"

Grandpa K asked, "Did you tell them you couldn't read when you went in?"

"No, we didn't tell them who we were or even which one of us were interested."

"Then it would have been hard to give you the information in an alternate form."

Well shit, he'd not thought of it that way.

Grandpa K said, "Maybe you should go back in and let them know the circumstances. Give them a chance to step up to the plate, so to speak."

"Hmm."

Grandpa K looked up at the sky. "Plenty of daylight for a two-hour drive. But you need to clean up a bit first. Take the small truck so it's not so hard to park." Then he moseyed on into the house and left Lloyd in the yard.

Tracy stomped up the stairs muttering all the way. "Stupid interfering man. Thinks he knows everything, and I don't know a damn thing. Maybe I did overdo it, a little. But him swooping in to save my poor stupid self was just too much."

She held her hands out that were covered in gauze, from wrist to fingertips. "I can't even function with this much protection. I barely got the stupid door open to get into the house. I can't do anything with my hands wrapped up like a mummy."

She dropped her hands down which caused them to throb, so she lifted them back up. "I realize my hands were bleeding and the antibacterial cream did make them feel better, after he about killed me by cleaning them. But blisters do that sometimes. It's not the first time I've had blisters pop and bleed and it probably won't be the last."

She got to her door and just looked at the knob. "He didn't need to be quite so obnoxious about my working too hard. Bossing me around being a pain. I'm not even able to get into my room. And how can I get out of these dirty clothes? I don't want to wear dirt-covered clothes. I want to take a shower. I'm sweaty and gross. And I can't do that with my hands wrapped."

She tried the door but couldn't come close to opening it. She couldn't get her hands around the knob. "I'll just have to undo them. Bossy, obnoxious, male. Thinks I'm too stupid. Hello, my life. Yeah, I was sweating. My face was probably red. And I was getting tired. No question about it. That doesn't mean he had to come in and take control of everything. Even taking me off the job site. Like he's in charge of me or something." She glared at the door and would have kicked it if it was hers.

"Need some help?" Tracy turned to find Meg behind her.

"Yeah, thanks. I didn't hear you."

"Hard to hear over your own furor."

Meg pushed the door open and followed Tracy into her room. "Let me give you a hand with some of those things you can't do with your hands all bandaged. I take it Lloyd was the one that pushed his will on you."

"Yes. You have sex with a guy, and he thinks he's in charge. How did you know it was Lloyd?"

Meg chuckled as she unbuttoned Tracy's shirt and helped her pull it off. "I recognize his handiwork. He's got a bit of a phobia about blisters getting infected. He'd have done the same with anyone. Although I imagine he does feel overprotective about you."

An irrational fear, okay, so that made sense about why he was so adamant. "What's the phobia about?"

Meg didn't look at her, but instead helped her out of her jeans. "It happened in the gold fields with his father and was a major reason they left there. But I think you should let Lloyd tell you about it."

Meg set Tracy's clothes in the hamper. "I'll take the gauze off so you can shower and when you're finished, I'll treat your hands to some bandages that you can function in. Tell me how you got the blisters."

"When we got out to the cabin, we could see that they'd delivered the dirt. So, we started transferring it up to the mine in the four-wheeler trailers. There is a lot of dirt, it's going to take days."

"Yes, I heard from Patricia that they will be here soon, with another young man. Travis is going to send some ranch hands, too. We can't spare them all with it being the end of calving season, but a few."

"Anyway, Brenda and I were working to help shovel and we sat down just for a minute to have some water and to rest our backs. Matt came over and was saying that since we're so little, and girls, if we needed to stop and rest it was fine. He sounded so condescending. Like because we were female, we couldn't do the job. Well, it raised our hackles, me and Brenda. So, we decided we'd show them."

"I imagine going to a ninety percent male school you've run into that a time or two."

"Oh yeah, there's a few on the faculty that still think women belong at home barefoot and pregnant. Some of the students start out that way, saying we're only there for an M.R.S degree, until we kick their ass in academics."

"So, it doesn't take much to set you off."

"I suppose not, we might have a hair trigger on that front. Anyway, I noticed that the gloves I was wearing were causing blisters."

"They're probably the wrong size," Meg said. "You didn't buy them yourself. Right?"

"No, the company gave them to me and yeah, you're right. They're too big."

"Well, that's one thing you need to put your foot down about. The company must supply you with proper equipment. They need to buy women's size work gloves for you and Brenda."

"Yeah, we'll take that up with them. We didn't think about it at the time. But the more we shoveled the worse it got with the gloves moving back and forth. At least on my hands. I assume Brenda's are the same, but I don't know for sure. I finally took them off and there were blisters but I thought we could keep going."

"Lloyd showed up about the time the blisters popped and started bleeding. He was furious. Ranting and raving about trying to kill myself. I was puffing, and my face was hot and probably bright red. I felt hot and sweaty, so I probably did overdo it."

Meg was examining her hands and lifted an eyebrow in response.

"But he's not in charge of me. He didn't have to be such a pain about it."

"If it was me, I might have paddled your butt, these are deep. Anyway, one of the things you'll learn about men is that they have a protector instinct. It's part of their makeup. You can argue until you are blue in the face but it's not going to change. It's no different than the way they are built physically."

Meg looked up at her. "Go shower. I'll get the first aid kit and we can finish this topic while I rebandage your hands. You won't be wielding a shovel any time soon."

The shower was painful, her hands screamed as she washed her body and her hair. She'd been foolish and her pride had caused pain. She finished her shower with gritted teeth and gingerly pulled on clothes, leaving her hair wrapped in a towel. Meg was waiting for her, she'd never had a motherly touch like this, at least not that she could remember, so she treasured it.

Tracy eagerly held out her hands, she wanted the antibacterial gel with the pain reliever in it back on the blisters.

Meg gently applied the ointment as she talked about the differences between a man and a woman. That they have broad shoulders and skinny hips, and women have wide hips and a slender waist. That men have more upper body strength, but a woman has better pain tolerance.

"Women are different than men. And that's okay. You don't have to try to be a man. Instead, you can be a strong woman. You have different strengths than a man, as do they. Learning to complement each other is a gift."

Tracy digested that, it made sense.

Meg said, "But you don't have to go toe to toe with a man about everything. Schoolwork, learning, intelligence, those things. Sure. Of course, we can handle it. But all of life is not a competition between the sexes. Lean into your strengths and let the men lean into theirs."

Meg had finished with her hands and turned her so she could help Tracy with her hair. "Matts married. I've never seen him be condescending towards his wife. Being married teaches a person, very intimately, the difference between a man and a woman. Maybe he wasn't trying to be condescending, maybe he was just being rational."

Tracy folded her arms across her chest. "I don't like that. But I suppose you might be right."

Meg pulled the comb through Tracy's long hair. "I've been married a long time. And I have a lot of sons. And I work on a ranch with a lot of men. So, I think I understand them. I know you go to school with a lot of them, but I'm not sure how much you've interacted with them."

"Not like you have, that's for sure," Tracy admitted. She was friendly with some of the guys on campus, but didn't really know them.

"You shouldn't be too hard on Lloyd. He hasn't been around a lot of women, so he doesn't necessarily know how to not be bossy. It's something he can learn, of course. But he does have to learn it. He's mostly been around men. There's only me and Emma that have been on the ranch that he's even had contact with. His mom died when he was a baby. He had his dad and his grandpa, but no real women for years. I'm probably the closest thing he's got to a female authority figure."

Meg set the comb down on the dresser. "You need to learn about men, and he needs to learn about women. And how the two of you interact. I know you're trying to prove yourself to the engineers, but don't go about it foolishly. You're equal in a lot of ways. Sometimes physically, you're not and that's okay. Because sometimes physically, they're not, for a different task."

"Thanks Meg, for the talk and the physical help."

Meg patted her on the shoulder. "It's okay. You've never really had anyone to show you the way and I'm happy to do so."

"Neither has Brenda for that matter."

"I imagine Thomas was a little bit more conscious of how to talk to Brenda than Lloyd was with you."

Tracy smiled. "Let's hope so. Because Brenda was as determined as I was. There are times we have to prove ourselves as capable, but maybe this wasn't one of them."

Meg smiled. "Maybe not."

CHAPTER 28

*L*loyd drove over the pass with single-minded determination, he was going to get this ironed out, one way or another, today. He was tired of living this way, the fight with sweet Tracy had pushed him right over the edge. Talking with Grandpa K had gotten him calmed down enough to make the drive. He'd be getting there late in the afternoon, but they would just have to deal with it.

He parked the ranch truck he'd borrowed in the parking lot and slammed the door. Shit, he needed to calm down, he couldn't go storming in there ready to raise hell. He took a moment to compose himself in the park in front of the building. He assumed when the school had first been built this grassy area had been a commons for the students to hang out in. Now it was a park with a playground and picnic tables, but he could almost feel the echoes of long ago, students eager to learn, ready to take on the world and make it a better place.

He sat on one of the large boulders and let the echoes from the past soothe him. Someone slapped him on the shoulder. He turned to find Steve grinning at him.

"Are you going to come in and let us talk you into attending?"

Lloyd wanted to deny it or act confidently but instead, he decided to be perfectly honest. "Steve, I just don't know if I've got what it takes. I was such a poor student growing up." Steve didn't say a word, just stood there listening. "I know it was because we didn't know about my dyslexia back then or how to manage it. I've compensated it now as an adult with reading apps and audio books."

Lloyd kicked at the dirt, as Steve waited patiently. Lloyd wished he'd say something, so he'd have someone to argue with. "Dammit, I just don't know if I've got the smarts to learn this." He waved his hand toward the building. "What if now after all my tricks and remedies, I'm still a piss poor student?"

Steve raised one eyebrow as if to say and what if you're not. Lloyd hoped that would be true, but… "I won't have anything to blame it on now. If I fail."

Steve didn't answer for a moment as the fear hung in the air, as if a living breathing monster. Finally, he said, "Lloyd, tell me one thing you've wanted to learn about since discovering your, what did you call it, tricks? One thing using your tricks that you wanted to learn but were incapable of doing so."

Lloyd could feel the rebellion rear its head. "Nothing. I've learned everything I've wanted to."

Steve grinned. "Exactly."

Lloyd chuckled. "Well, that was sneaky."

"Yep, I've learned a thing or two myself. Now get your ass in the school and apply for fall semester. Martha will take your application verbally and enter it into the computer. Saves her time trying to read chicken scratch."

An hour later Lloyd walked out of the building with a

flash drive. Everything he needed to know was in digital format, so he didn't have to struggle through trying to read paper documents. He was enrolled as a student and the mine reclamation company had already paid his tuition.

He was scared shitless, but also as proud as he could be. He couldn't wait to tell Tracy.

If she was speaking to him.

TRACY PACED HER ROOM. LLOYD HAD NOT COME IN FOR dinner. She'd gone over to the bunkhouse to talk to him but was informed he wasn't there. Where had he gone? Was he breaking up with her? People in her life never stuck around, so it was probably over between them.

She had to fight to keep that idea at bay. Tracy wasn't going to give in, she wasn't a child anymore, one who had no choice in the matter. He would at least be her friend again, even if they weren't lovers and she could handle that, maybe, probably.

When there was a knock on the door, she called out, "Come in."

Lloyd opened the door and she felt enormous relief to see the joy on his face. Holding up her bandaged hands she said, "Even though Meg made the bandages smaller I still have trouble with doorknobs." It was a lame statement to make but better than just standing there stupidly.

"I had to come share my news with my best girl." He dropped a shopping bag on the floor and shut the door behind him.

That sounded good, her being his girl. She felt herself relax even more.

"After I dropped you off here at the house I went to

Grandville and to the reclamation certification school. I've been a mess because of that school and the fact I couldn't even read the papers they gave us."

"Oh, I should have helped you with them. I didn't think…"

"Never mind that. I was pissed off that they hadn't provided them in a format I could use, but Grandpa K reminded me we didn't tell them who I was, so they would know to do that. So, I went back to see what they would do if I told them who I was."

He held up a flash drive with a grin. "Guess it helped. I ran into Steve before I went in, and he pointed out a few things and then told me to get my ass in there. So, I did, the woman at the counter, Martha, took my application verbally and entered it right into the computer."

Tracy felt the happiness radiating off of him and it filled her heart, too.

"Then she gave me the flash drive that includes the start date and class schedule and told me to be back in time for orientation. With the reclamation company sponsoring me, I didn't have to do anything else. I've already been accepted based on Steve, Patricia, Matt, and Connor's recommendation."

Tracy couldn't stand it one minute longer and flew into his arms. "I'm so happy for you."

He gave her a huge bear hug, then lifted her chin up and kissed the stuffing out of her.

When they finally broke apart, he asked, "Want to be my roommate?"

Her heart lifted in joy; she wouldn't be all alone this year like she'd been dreading. "I would love to be your roommate."

He swept her up and carried her to the bed, after many

long and steamy kisses, he pulled back. "It's probably too soon, but I have to ask. Would you consider being my permanent roommate?"

Her breath caught and she squeaked out, "What are you asking me?"

"I'm asking you to marry me. I want to be your forever man and we can have a forever family of our own. I'm asking you to me my forever woman. I love you, Tracy. I want to spend the rest of my life with you."

Tears flooded her eyes, and a huge lump filled her throat, she couldn't speak, could barely breathe, but she could nod, and she could smile. He kissed her again and her throat opened. "Lloyd, I would be so happy to have you as my forever man. I love you; I was so scared you were done with me."

"Done? I'm just getting started. You're my heart, you give me courage to believe in myself. I can hardly wait to take this next step with you by my side."

She poked him in the side. "You'll have to learn not to be so bossy."

"I'll work on that, if you'll work on not being so stubborn."

"Deal. What's in the bag?"

"Every size and shape of glove I could find in Denver. No more ill-fitting gloves for you, my love."

She laughed, "But I only need one pair."

"I didn't know what size, so I got one of each. After you find the correct one, and Brenda does too, we can take the rest back when we go to look for somewhere to live for the school year." He shook his head. "I can hardly believe I said that, let alone plan to get more education."

"Formal education. You never stopped learning."

"Hmm, you're right about that."

179

"Now kiss me. Enough of this talking."

With a grin he covered her lips and loved her very thoroughly until she was boneless. She fell asleep wrapped in his arms. Her last thought was she would be spending her life just like that, and it was the best plan ever.

EPILOGUE

*L*loyd put the last box of Tracy's books in the back of the new-to-him Chevy Equinox. It was the first vehicle he'd ever owned; he and Tracy had picked it out one weekend. They'd debated between the equinox and a truck. He'd always driven trucks, the ranch trucks, but they'd finally decided on the SUV. They didn't own it outright, but he'd put down a large deposit from the money he'd had in the bank, so the payments were small.

The whole family was there to see them off. He'd probably not be back on the ranch to live. After graduation he and Tracy would get a trailer, maybe one they could pull with the Equinox to start, while they moved between job sites.

His life had changed forever and with the beautiful woman by his side, he couldn't be happier. She wore his ring and they planned to be married on the ranch once they had both graduated. Everyone they loved lived on the ranch, so it was a logical choice. He already had their honeymoon booked. They were spending three weeks in southern California, where they would enjoy Disneyland, Universal Studios, and wherever else they felt like going. But that was nearly a year away, they were just starting on this new endeavor.

Lloyd and Tracy were hugged by every member of the family. He'd been surprised when each member handed him an envelope with a comment on using it for the future. He'd tried to argue, but Grandpa K had set him straight.

"You're our family, son, don't deprive us of seeing you off with a bit of extra cash."

"Yes, sir. I appreciate it."

"Good, use it wisely. Except for once in a while, where you use it foolishly, think of us then."

Lloyd had found it particularly hard to say goodbye to Meg. "You've been the only mother I've ever known. I'll miss you most of all."

She ruffled his hair. "I have a phone; you have a phone. I expect regular updates, but even more than that I expect you to call me when you can't figure out your girl. I've told her to do the same when she can't understand you. I'm female but I've raised and lived with a lot of men. I've got opinions, many of them, so use them when you need to."

Lloyd hugged her tight. "I will. I'll call, or we can facetime."

"Good, now get on with your life and remember you're always welcome here." She glanced around then said slyly, "We've got an extra plot of land you can build on should you want to live in something besides a trailer."

He laughed. "I might just take you up on that."

"Good, now scoot."

Tracy slid in next to him and he handed her his envelopes.

She said, "They all gave you envelopes, too?"

"What do you mean 'too'?"

"They gave me some," she said softly.

He'd never felt so well loved as he did at that moment. "They are all crazy you know."

"Travis told me, that when we get tired of living in a trailer, they have a plot of land for us to build a home on. I nearly sobbed."

He shook his head. "Meg told me the same."

Tracy said, "I guess I have my forever family, after all this time."

"You do, and we'll build one of our own. I wouldn't mind having a home base on the ranch. If we're working over here on the western slope, it would be easy to drive to a job site."

"Or at least to come back on weekends and holidays."

"We'll look into that after we graduate." He squeezed her hand as he turned onto the highway heading toward Denver.

"Goody, now we're off to our learning adventure, together. Me and my forever man."

Contentment and excitement filled him, and Tracy's sigh conveyed she was feeling the same.

THE END

The series continues in Just as You Are, Ramona's story.
If you enjoyed this story, please leave a review on your
favorite retailer, Bookbub, or Goodreads.
Thanks so much!

ALSO BY SHIRLEY PENICK

Ted and Tammy's story

The Author's Lady Librarian: Lake Chelan #11

Patty Anne and Gideon's story

The Fire Chief's Surprise: Lake Chelan #12

Greg and Sandy's short story

Hello Again: Lake Chelan #13

Janet and Everett's story

(Previously part of the Goodbye Doesn't Mean Forever anthology)

Three's a Crowd: Lake Chelan #14

Kyle and Samantha's story

(Previously part of the Valentine Kisses anthology)

A Heart Knows: Lake Chelan #15

Michelle and Peter's story

(Previously part of the Heatin' Up Steel City anthology)

BURLAP AND BARBED WIRE SERIES

Colorado Cowboys

A Cowboy for Alyssa: Burlap and Barbed Wire #1

Beau and Alyssa's story

Taming Adam: Burlap and Barbed Wire #2

Adam and Rachel's story

Tempting Chase: Burlap and Barbed Wire #3

Chase and Katie's story

Roping Cade: Burlap and Barbed Wire #4

Cade and Summer's story

Trusting Drew: Burlap and Barbed Wire #5

Drew and Lily's story

Emma's Rodeo Cowboy: Burlap and Barbed Wire #6

Emma and Zach's story

SADDLES AND SECRETS SERIES

Wyoming Wranglers

The Lawman: Saddles and Secrets #1

Maggie Ann and John's story

The Watcher: Saddles and Secrets #2

Christina and Rob's story

The Rescuer: Saddles and Secrets #3

Milly and Tim's story

The Vacation: Saddles and Secrets Short Story #4

Andrea and Carl Ray's story

(Previously part of the Getting Wild in Deadwood anthology)

The Neighbor: Saddles and Secrets #5

Terri and Rafe's story

HELLUVA ENGINEER SERIES

Helluva Engineer

Patricia and Steve's story

Christmas at the Rockin' K: Helluva Engineer #2

Brenda and Thomas's story

Her Forever Man: Helluva Engineer #3

Tracy and Lloyd's story

ABOUT THE AUTHOR

What does a geeky math nerd know about writing romance?

That's a darn good question. As a former techy I've done everything from computer programming to international trainer. Prior to college I had lots of different jobs and activities that were so diverse, I was an anomaly.

None of that qualifies me for writing novels. But I have some darn good stories to tell and a lot of imagination.

I have lived in Colorado, Hawaii and currently reside in Washington. Going from two states with 340 days of sun to a state with 340 days of clouds, I had to do something to perk me up. And that's when I started this new adventure called author. Joining the Romance Writers of America and two local chapters, helped me learn the craft quickly and has been a ton of fun.

My family consists of two grown children, their spouses, two adorable grand-daughters, and one grand dog. My favorite activity is playing with my granddaughters!

When the girls can't play with their amazing grandmother, my interests are reading and writing, yay! I started reading at a young age with the Nancy Drew mysteries and have continued to be an avid reader my whole life. My favorite reading material is romance, but occasionally if other stories creep into my to-be-read pile, I don't kick them out.

Some of the strange jobs I have held are a carnation grower's worker, a trap club puller, a pizza hut waitress, a software engineer, an international trainer, and a business program manager. I took welding, drafting and upholstery in high school, a long time ago, when girls didn't take those classes, so I have an eclectic bunch of knowledge and experience.

And for something really unusual… I once had a raccoon as a pet.

Join with me as I tell my stories, weaving real tidbits from my life in with imaginary ones. You'll have to guess which is which. It will be a hoot!

Contact me:
www.shirleypenick.com
To sign up for Shirley's Monthly Newsletter, sign up on my website or send email to shirleypenick@outlook.com, subject newsletter.

Follow me:

facebook.com/ShirleyPenickAuthorFans

twitter.com/shirley_penick

instagram.com/shirleypenickauthor

bookbub.com/authors/shirley-penick

goodreads.com/shirleypenick